Retired On Love

All or Nothing Book One

RENÉE A. MOSES

GussyFlo Publishing

To my babies, Angelina, Zoë, and Ryan, we have been through A LOT the last three years. I thank you for your love and patience as I navigate this new chapter of ours. God got us. We're in this together. Love you.

To Aunt Cathy (Aunt Maya LOL), remember that dream I had about you being married and hooking me up with your husband's nephew? This it right here.

To Gustavia (Moses), we did it again!

ONE

Khaliyah

THE SUBTLE BURNING of my cheek awakened me. Groaning, I rolled to my side. Tossing the covers to the empty side of my bed, I let the ceiling fan's coolness wake me even more. The naked beige walls used to wear pictures that depicted the disguise of love over the last decade. My eyes roamed over them, searching for the nail holes, visualizing the framed photos now in storage.

"Khaliyah, get it together. God has other plans. Let it go."

Christian was at his condo, doing whatever a divorced man would do. Shit, he lived that life before anything was ever finalized. I got what I needed from the marriage, and he kept the rest, including this big house and everything in it. If my builder hadn't encountered delays, we'd be there instead of here. Every turn reminded me of the past, but I took a slow breath, embracing the present and future.

I willed myself out of bed after glancing at the time on the clock on my nightstand. Not even seven a.m. Two and a half hours of sleep would get me through the day. I took care of my business in the bathroom, got on my knees to spend time with God, and then decided to finish some work before the kids woke up.

Before I made it to the kitchen for some coffee, the doorbell rang. I reached the door and yanked it open, alarming the older woman on the other side. "Who are you? And why are you at my house this early?"

She cleared her throat, possibly excusing my rudeness. It was too damn early to mistakenly knock on the wrong door. "Hi, I'm Marie from Dreamy Rental Agency. I have a seven o'clock meeting with Christian and Kaitlyn."

"Kaitlyn?"

I understood my name wasn't the easiest to pronounce, but it didn't look like Kaitlyn. "I think you have the wrong address." I shut the door, and in a split second, I processed the other name she mentioned. I pulled the door open again. "Wait, Christian who? What's the last name?"

Marie checked her phone, swiping a few times to verify. "Luke. It's Christian Luke and Kaitlyn Parr. I believe they are the owners."

"What the hell?" I asked under my breath, rubbing my temples. "Give me a minute. I need to... Hold on." I closed the door, still not understanding what was happening.

I rushed to my room, passing Ashtyn on the way. "Who is that, Ma?"

"Somebody for your dad. Lemme call him and see 'cause I'd be damned if this nigga didn't—" I had to stop myself before I placed any worry on my son. The divorce did enough of that on its own. His father, giving me full custody, delivered a harsher blow. I didn't want to make it worse.

"Go lie back down if you can. I'll get this handled. Okay?"

"Okay, Ma."

I gave him a pound and continued toward my room to get my phone. I had missed calls and texts, all from Christian. I worked late last night and turned my notifications off.

Instead of reading the messages, I called him. "What?" he answered, rude as hell.

"Why is there a woman at my door from a rental agency?"

"You mean my door? I got the house in the settlement."

If I could slap him through the phone, I would. "Whatever the fuck it is, why is she here? I told you we'd be here a little longer because of the builder delays."

"You did."

"Christian, what are you doing?"

"I'm on my way. I told Marie I'd be a couple of minutes late."

Chirp. Chirp

Someone had opened a door that triggered the entry security alert. I hurried to the front, knowing damn well it wasn't my kids or Marie. I came face-to-face with a long-legged black female in my foyer. The key was still in her hand.

"Who are you? How did you get into my house?"

"Sweetheart, when was the last time you checked the deed?" She sneered. "This is *my* house. Why are you still in it?" Her hand dramatically rose to her hip and rested there.

"Hello?" Christian's voice came over my speaker phone. "Can you hear me?"

"Yes, love. We both can." The woman answered him.

My free hand trembled. I was two seconds from charging at her for her audacity alone. Not jealousy. Her arrogant ass walked in here like my family didn't dwell here for years. I'd never seen this giraffe ass bitch a day in my life, yet she stood as if she knew me.

"Christian Luke, you have one gotdamn minute to get yo' trifling ass here because somebody is leaving in an ambulance."

I took two steps toward the woman, and Aubrey's voice reeled me back to reality, where I was a respectable woman and a mother of three. Three of whom were still in this house.

"Mommy! It's loud." Aubrey held onto her stuffed bunny. "I can't sleep anymore."

"Mommy is so sorry. Go brush your teeth and put on some clothes."

"Okay," she responded softly. Aubrey woke up a little more when she laid eyes on the woman near the front door. "Who is that, Mommy?"

"No one important, babes," I informed her in the most gentle tone I could muster. "Go get ready." I kissed her cheek.

As soon as she turned around, the unidentified bitch opened her mouth. "We'll see how unimportant I am when Christian gets here."

Jesus, take the wheel because I'm about to run this hoe over. Body count aside, she was still a hoe for walking in here the way she did. I slowly counted down from ten in my head with my eyes closed.

The woman's footsteps clacked too many times for me to keep my eyes shut. She headed toward the kitchen.

"Uh-unh. Where are you going?" I quickly met her before she could go any further, raising my hand in protest.

"I'm examining my new home. I need to see how I can remove the...tacky." She stepped closer to her original spot by the front door. The heifer looked down at me figuratively and literally before saying, "I have to impress potential renters, sweetheart." My spiritual enemy was working hard to have my ass in jail. Every time she opened her mouth, I envisioned my fist busting it.

Without backing down, I stepped closer yet remained a respectful distance. Her long, toned arms couldn't reach me. Looking her dead in her eyes, I made myself clear. "You must think this is a game. Get the fuck out! I don't give a shit what you and Christian got going on. Yo' ass can wait outside for him."

Her shoulders barely bounced. "Tuh! All it will take is one phone call and your ghetto ass will be on the street like you belong."

Yeah, nope! *Jesus, I tried.*

"Bitch, you won't be alive long enough to dial the muthafucking number." I moved toward her, fist balled and ready for contact.

Before I could make another stride, I heard, "Mom! What's going on?" Ashtyn asked with enough alert in his eyes for me to remember who I was.

Both my sons had walked into the foyer fully awake. As much as I wanted to drag this bitch, I still had to maintain some level of decorum. Children can sober you up quickly.

"Your mother is being—" the elongated female started.

"Nah, bitch. You will not speak to my kids. Like I said, get out. This is your final warning."

It was mine, too. Any more, and these kids would see Mommy in a different light. I'd have to apologize later.

Her brow hiked as if she'd dare to try me, but she made the best decision for her future and mine when she turned around and walked out the door. I locked the door again. If for nothing else but to slow Christian down whenever he got here.

"Ma, who was that?" Aydyn inquired for an answer I no longer needed or cared to know.

I inhaled and exhaled with a prayer in my head. Looking at my sons with love and patience, I told them, "Boys, get dressed and pack your things. We're leaving today."

Ashtyn's confusion matched mine internally. "But I thought—"

"Look, I will explain what I can in the car. Help your sister get her things. We gotta go."

Aydyn looked like he wanted to say something, but once our eyes met, he changed his mind.

Thank God.

The boys left me alone in the foyer, where I went over several scenarios of how my ex-husband would meet his fire-dwelling, two-horned, enemy-of-God maker. Christian had done and said a lot of crazy, unbelievable shit over the past fifteen years but this...

Hell, I didn't even know what this was.

In minutes, we were packed up and ready. Our things were already in suitcases since we were supposed to leave days ago, but my new house was three weeks behind schedule. Everything we were taking had already moved to Houston. The one week I planned on staying at my aunt's place has now extended to a month.

Christian gave the impression that he didn't care when I told him about the changes as soon as I received the information. I still assumed we'd stay in the house a little longer. To now witness how much he didn't give a fuck was enough for me to remove myself and my kids from the situation before it became something I couldn't take back.

Jail was my only plausible option with all this. Christian had me so fucked up, but I shook it off. After getting dressed, I prayed in my closet for a few minutes, and the boys helped me put our bags in the car. They asked a million and one questions. I only had one answer.

"We're moving today."

During the three-hour drive to Houston, I'd have time to inform my aunt and grandparents that we'd be on our way for good.

TWO

Airen

ANOTHER DAY, another venture someone wants me to be a part of. People didn't understand how to take no for an answer anymore. If you say no to one thing, they'd try to find another way to make you say yes.

My days of agreeing to any and everything were over. I had better things to do with my life and my precious time. Nothing was better than taking care of my baby girl.

I looked at my agent, who sat across the table. Her eyes were glued to the screen with a goofy ass smile, like she'd discovered how to monetize blinking.

That woman talked up this deal with a rep from my former employer as if it'd be the opportunity I couldn't pass up. Unbeknownst to her, I was about to fumble the ball with her expectations. Not something I'd do on the field, but real life proved to be an entirely different ball game.

I'd spent so much time on the road and working. I'd missed too many firsts in my daughter's life. I'd missed all the signs with her mother. That milk had spilled, spoiled, and stained. I couldn't do a thing about it now. I'd at least try to make it up to my little girl.

"Mr. Landry, I appreciate your time and hope you will consider this offer. We'd love to work with you."

I kept my head steady to not give any inkling that I'd consider a damn thing. August watched and waited for me to respond. When I didn't, her eyes squinted and her mouth tightened. She returned her attention to the screen when Mr. Schmegler cleared his throat. He probably expected the same type of enthusiasm as August displayed.

"We will discuss your offer and get back to you soon. Thank you so much for thinking about Airen for your show."

"Of course," he said, less enthusiastically. "Talk soon." The TV returned to its home screen.

"What the fuck was that, Airen?" August stared me down before she expelled all of her stored air. I clasped my hands on the table, blinking slowly. "Damn! You could have pretended to be interested."

Kissing my teeth at her unnecessary attitude, I let her have it. "You could pretend you know me well enough not to drag me here for this. I'm not doing it. What the hell I look like hosting a show with that clown? I'm good, dawg."

"Look, you will be a Hall of Famer one day. You didn't even sign on for the last contract when *we* agreed you would. I'm trying to get us paid. You worked so hard to accomplish all that you have. Why not eat from it while you can? It's a sports talk show!"

"August, I love and respect you, but I told you I'm done with them muthafuckas. They don't give a shit about me and the life I have to live when I step off the field. I couldn't care less about being in the hall of fame. It won't reverse time and fix all that they had a hand in fucking up."

"I'm bout to take off this damn stiletto and stab you with it. You cannot blame the NFL for what happened. Fame is a drug. No one knows who will become an addict."

"Man, miss me with that. You get what I mean."

"You mean you are misdirecting your anger? You need to blame the only person responsible for the actions that put you in the position you're in right now. These muthafuckas, as you say, wanna throw money at you for something you're naturally gifted at. Something you used to love more than anything."

"Those days are over. I don't want to be in front of any cameras or the public eye ever again. I love my daughter more than anything. Speaking of, I need to get back to her. Unc has plans."

"A'ight, Airen. If you say so."

"I definitely say so."

"Whatever. I got work to do. Thank goodness you aren't my only client anymore. Maybe my first, but if I didn't rep others, I'd make no money since you turn down every opportunity."

"Then give me something I can get behind. I don't want the vultures coming for me. I wanna chill. It's not like I need the money."

"Well, lil' folk like me do. Anyway, I'll see you later. Kiss my boo for me."

"Will do."

<hr>

MY UNCLE TOOK my daughter to the park while I had my meeting. Our nanny, Annise, resigned two months ago to have her baby, and I hadn't searched for her replacement. With so much time on my hands, I realized I was throwing money away. My baby girl turned five and only had a few weeks before school. She'd been homeschooled for pre-k with Annise.

After the years we had, I wanted to keep my little girl close. Sending her to preschool so soon after everything didn't seem like the right move. With her mother gone, Annise came through at the right time. One recommendation from August and a great interview later, I hired her on the spot. The original plan was for Annise to work with us for three years. I figured I'd be able to manage by then. An unexpected pregnancy turned my three-year plan into one and a half.

Lately, I have relied on my uncle and his wife regarding my daughter. Meetings were the only time I needed their help. Once August accepted I wasn't going back to the NFL in any capacity, nor would I enter the spotlight for any reason; we'd be good.

"There's my baby!" I waited in the kitchen doorway as Ari ran toward me.

"Daddy! You're back!" she hugged me tightly.

"Wuzzup, Uncle Roach." My uncle's smile quickly dissipated right before he swung. I darted out of reach.

"That's why yo' momma ugly."

"You gonna talk about your sister like that?"

"Yep, cuz she passed them same looks to you."

I stepped back as I laughed. He always had something to say about my looks. "That hate game is strong today. Do I need to get some Raid?"

"Boy!" he caught me upside the head. Unc favored Carl Payne, and his hat game was just as impressive. I teased, calling him Cole from Martin, but his character, Cockroach from The Cosby Show riled him up more.

Ari sat at the table, giggling at us while she ate her snack. After we called a truce, we joined her. I took a few of her goldfish and popped them into my mouth.

"How was the meeting?" Unc inquired.

I rolled my eyes, completely forgetting about it after entering the serenity of my dwelling. The outside world left my thoughts every time I crossed the threshold.

"Auggie somehow thought I'd be up for co-hosting a new show on ESPN. That nigga Roland is the other host."

"Whaaat?! Didn't he get hurt right after you retired?"

"He did. Out for good."

"Damn. Whose bright idea was it to put you two on a show together?"

"Somebody who lost their rabid ass mind."

Unc cleared his throat. "Well, what are you going to do? Yes, you have all the money you'll ever need, but nephew, you can't sit in the house for the rest of your life."

The dreaded question on everybody's minds made it seem like I had a deadline to figure it out. All I could tell him was the truth. "I don't know." That answer almost felt like a lie, since there had been one thing heavy on my mind to do. I let go of my fear of saying it out loud. "I keep returning to the rec center idea for young athletes, but..."

Unc leaned back in his chair, narrowing his eyes. "What's the pause for?"

I revealed the biggest hurdle in my idea and the cause for my hesitation. "I'd have to get other people involved, raise funds, and—"

"And come out of hiding." The man hit it on the head, but I wouldn't let him have that satisfaction.

I sucked my teeth. "I ain't in hiding."

"Boy, you put your house in my name so no one could track the records to you. What do you call that?"

I smiled to avoid laughing at myself. "Man, it's not even in your name anymore. I was only protecting my daughter and myself. The less people know, the better."

"After the ordeal you've experienced, I understand. At some point, you'll have to face the world again. If for nothing else, show that it didn't break you."

"I don't owe them anything. I'm good."

"You right." Unc sighed as his cheek rose. "Well, the missus and I are having a little get-together soon and would love for you to come. Kids are welcome. There will be some there for my little angel to play with." He rubbed Ari's arm.

"Would you like that?" he asked her. Ari answered with a smile and a nod.

THREE

Khaliyah

After writing another journal entry, I chilled in bed with my mini-me. Aubrey watched *My Little Pony* as I zoned in and out. The pressure was on for me to scale my business, and I'd need to hire help to do it successfully.

PopPop always instilled in me to have multiple streams of income. He said to never trust what seemed like a sure thing. These folks at the top didn't give a damn about pulling the rug from the people at the bottom if that rug cost too much to keep. He was right.

Child support was enough to complement what I made on my own. I wanted to scale up to not need Christian's money for anything.

"The food's here," Aunt Maya hollered from downstairs.

I rounded up my litter and headed down. The boys flew down the stairs like they hadn't eaten in days. I didn't know where their food went because both were slim and taller than me. They were lanky like their dad, but I was glad they didn't inherit my height. Now, Aubrey might not be so lucky. She held my hand as we walked to the kitchen.

"It smells so good!" I took it all in as the spices filled the area.

Ashtyn and Aydyn opened their bags of snow crab,

shrimp, corn, and potatoes. Aunt Maya wanted to go out to eat, but Uncle Rochon wouldn't get home until later. He was helping his nephew do some yard work. Auntie was stuck with me, and I wasn't in the mood to go anywhere.

"Y'all come out here with that food. I got the fans going. It feels good now," Aunt Maya called from the screened-in patio.

We took our bags and joined her. As hot as it was, those industrial-looking fans made a vast difference. The boys sat at the outdoor table and turned on the projector for the wall TV. Aubrey sat with me and Aunt Maya, since I had to peel her shrimp and crack her crab. Lord knows I'd be so glad when she could do it herself.

"We're missing one thing. I'll be right back." My aunt rushed into the house.

I finished preparing Aubrey's food and gave her my phone so she could watch her shows while we ate peacefully. Aunt Maya returned with a bottle of pineapple wine.

Her silly grin tickled me. "Do you have to drink with every meal?" I asked.

"No, but I want to. Therefore, I will do just that. I don't understand why you're complaining. You need a drink."

"If I keep drinking every time I get stressed, I'ma be an alcoholic."

"Girl, please. You have self-control. Now, help me drink this bottle." She handed me a full glass of wine, which I gladly took. "Enjoy!" She raised her glass to mine as we carefully clinked them together.

"Ma! You ain't see that? Ashtyn threw a shrimp shell at me," Aydyn yelled.

I rolled my eyes for maybe the thousandth time today. Having sons back to back was about the craziest idea ever. Technically, Aydyn came unexpectedly. Hell, none of them were planned. But I didn't expect to be pregnant two years in a row. Then, to have a surprise baby once Ashtyn was in the second grade! I thought I had it made when both boys were in school. My grandmother forbade me from permanently closing my womb with her: "You can't predict how you'll feel about it in a few years. You're still young." Yeah, whatever.

"Stop playing with your damn food. You're too old for me to even be saying that, Ashtyn. Pick it up."

All I heard was the loudest sucking of the teeth sound before he picked up the food he'd thrown. I was ready to knock him upside his head when I heard him mumble something. He was lucky that Aunt Maya stopped me by resting her hand on my forearm.

"Y'all eat and be nice. Your mother has enough to deal with than having to make y'all scrub the furniture and the ground with toothbrushes if you spill or splatter seafood juice anywhere."

Ashtyn and Aydyn looked wearily at their great-aunt, then back at each other. "See what you did?" Ashtyn said.

Aydyn's head jerked back. "Me? You started it."

"But you always gotta run to Mommy. You big baby."

"I'm not a—"

"Boys! Enough! Damn!" I raised my voice enough to put an end to it.

"Sorry," they said, one after the other.

"Girl, y'all are something else." Aunt Maya sipped her wine. "So, are you excited about the house? You've got only a few weeks left, right?"

"Just about. I'm so sick of these delays. We were supposed to be in there before school started. This is their first time going to public school in years. I wanted everything to be perfect. Plus, Aubrey's going to kindergarten. I planned on having her room all decorated with a little desk area and everything."

"Oh, please. Those things will come. I'm sure you'll be

glad to get your days back. I couldn't imagine homeschooling all my kids. Hell, they finished school and left me behind."

"Northern California, Minnesota, and Colorado. I'm sure your kids left because they wanted to escape this close-to-hell heat."

Auntie bobbed her head in agreement. "Ooooh, I can't wait to see my grands next week. They are the reason we're putting this little shindig together. Rochon done invited all of his friends. It was supposed to be a family thing."

I shrugged, understanding my uncle's reasoning. "His friends are his family."

Aunt Maya rolled her eyes before swallowing. "They are."

For a minute or two, the only sounds came from smacking lips and the movie the boys had put on. I finally looked up and caught her watching me. My expression asked the question before my lips could. She answered with, "Roshon also invited his nephew."

I raised my hand to block any response. "Y'all better not be planning nothing because I'm done. I have my babies, business, and family to keep me occupied for a lifetime."

Auntie tilted her head toward me, eyes darting straight to mine. "That's what you say now."

"I'm saying it, and I mean it. I'm done," I dared to declare, even though she clearly felt otherwise. "I should have stayed with Gammy," I teased. Her gasp had me leaning over, laughing.

I meant what I said. My responsibilities and priorities were my babies. Provide and be happy by my damn self were the only goals in every department of my life. Auntie needed to get on board.

Uncle Rochon volunteered to watch my babies when Aunt Maya claimed we needed a little girl time. I texted my sister from another mister, Karina, and she met us at a local restaurant my aunt frequented. Luckily, she pulled up a couple of minutes after we did.

"Either she was out already, or she still drives like a bat out of hell," Aunt Maya said when Karina headed toward the car.

Once inside, we chose a bar table in the corner. All I wanted to do was relax and not think about life.

My bestie cleared her throat loud as hell after we placed our orders. "Auntie?" she asked. Aunt Maya perked up from studying the wine list, giving Karina all her attention. "Did you hear about Christian getting engaged?"

"Say what now?" Aunt Maya leaned to the side dramatically.

I rolled my eyes, then closed them again to say a quick prayer. "We didn't come here to talk about that fool, Karina. Damn! If I don't care, you shouldn't."

Aunt Maya's gaze fell on me. "You don't care? You should if she's gonna be around your kids. Do you know the woman?"

I blew out the last breath of peace I'd held onto. This conversation was inevitable. I could admit that talking about things helped. Lately, I only wanted to talk to God. I loved my family, but what could they do to help me?

After explaining what happened my last morning in our old house and learning about this other woman joining the couples' group we used to hang with when I was married, the ladies mouths were on the table. Admitting that my ex-husband already had a woman lined up before he demanded a divorce was embarrassing. The woman walking into "my" house because she indeed owned the place was something I wished to forget.

We divorced a little over a year ago, and he was already

getting married. It explained so much when I learned of his relationship. Not that he was a very present father, however, when we split, it was like he forgot he had kids.

The random texts claiming he loved them didn't go far after a while. We sort of developed a new normal without him. Watching my kids long for him and never having their expressed feelings acknowledged broke my heart the most. So, our choice to move away was the easiest family decision to make.

My ex was dead to me. However, the ladies hadn't gone through the discovery and healing process like I had. All of this was news to them because of my embarrassment. I stayed all those years. I ignored many signs for the sake of keeping my family together. In the end, I still came up short. His loss. My kids were worth the sacrifice.

For the rest of the supposed relaxing night, I listened to Karina and Aunt Maya curse Christian, plot to do bodily harm, and worse. As much as I wanted to avoid this conversation, I needed it. We laughed and drank until they claimed they were done with the topic.

Thank you, Father. Now, please help our inebriated behinds get home safely.

FOUR

Airen

I GRABBED four beers from the fridge, then returned to the men debating the role of a wife. I stayed out of these arguments because I didn't care enough to even have an opinion. Romantic relationships weren't in the cards for me after Mercy. No one would ever get that close to me again. I couldn't afford to even open that door in my life.

Uncle Rochon and Nick were on one side, while Izak fought hard on the other. Once I handed each man a bottle, I sat and listened to the back and forth.

"Son, I understand you are young," Unc started the way he always did when he was about to school you. "I'm giving you that. However, you cannot tell me that your future wife is going to go for the barefoot and pregnant mess. When my wife and I got married, we agreed we'd be a team. No one person was responsible for one thing, and the other wasn't.

"Now, I don't mean by providing I pay the bills. I'm a man; that's just how I'm built. If she didn't want to work, she wouldn't have to, but there would be a limit on what we could do and afford if she didn't. When we met, she had grown children. We had successful businesses. I would never ask her to give up everything she'd built to wait on me hand and foot like I'm royalty and she's my servant."

"I hear you, but let's say y'all met when y'all were younger and she didn't work and stayed home with kids. You wouldn't expect her to cook and clean on her own?" Izak asked.

I already knew where my uncle stood, so this would be a long conversation. Izak and Nick got in yesterday. We played together for years in Arizona until I stepped away. One damn game forced them into retirement from the NFL after incurring career ending injuries.

My boys came here for a business meeting with August. She wanted us together to discuss a plan for our unemployed asses. We had side businesses to grow our income steadily. I had a few anonymous YouTube channels with sports clips and those popular funny fails clips. When a buddy introduced it, I thought he was crazy, but by the end of the first year, I considered him a genius. Who knew video compilations would be so lucrative?

"No! If she took care of the kids, her ass would be as tired as you'd be working all day. If food wasn't on the table, I'd take my capable ass in the kitchen and hook something up." Unc tried to school Izak, yet the message went in one canal and out the other.

"Facts," Nick added. "Then she'd be so grateful that she might hook something up in the bedroom later." Those two shared a look that told us it was all worth it.

Izak clapped his hands loud as hell to shut that down. "Bro, I'm not cooking or cleaning if I have a woman at home. What the hell is she there for if she ain't doing all the domestic shit?"

"Nigga, just stay single. You ain't gone get it." Nick picked up a pack of cards from the table in front of him. I assumed he was done with it and wanted to move on to something else. I was with him.

"Y'all sound crazy." Izak wouldn't let it go. When he thought he was right, he got like that. "There are women who would gladly take care of me, the housework, and the kids if I paid all the bills."

"I'm not saying they won't, youngin'. But don't expect to never have to lift a finger and assist with the housework. It's your house too. You're not marrying a maid. If you treat your woman like that, she will walk out on your ass. Women need to be valued. If that's what she wants to contribute, then more power to her. If not..."

"If not, then my ass ain't checking for her, no way," Izak finished.

That nigga had two relationships fall apart because of this same mentality. He didn't have to do anything but work. He didn't even take out the trash. Both of his women had full-time jobs he'd convinced them to quit, and they ended up regretting it in the end.

Because of my uncle, I knew better than to expect my lady to do every single thing at home. I was considerate when I was married. I cooked when time permitted, helped around the house, and took care of Ariyah so Mercy could have long breaks. I never wanted my wife to feel neglected or unappreciated.

I valued and honored my wife. I pampered her myself or by the way of professionals. Her self-care was crucial if I expected her to hold down the fort when I wasn't there. Even then, I paid for her to have help. Taking care of a home was a lot of work when you had children. If I wanted a little something when I got home, preserving her energy became a must. Selfish, maybe, but before she left me for the world, it worked.

Nick snapped his fingers like he'd just remembered something. "Yo, didn't you say something about August tryna throw you on a show with Roland? How's that supposed to work?"

"Shit, it ain't and it won't. I shut that down immediately.

She knows me better than that." My mouth tightened at the assumption that I'd even entertain it.

Public popularity didn't appeal to me like it did for most. I'd had my share of the spotlight and that shit was for the birds. It stole my wife, lied about me, and ran with whatever made the best ratings. A show on any network would only bring back everything I'd worked so hard to separate myself from.

As much as I want to be an adult about the situation and forgive all involved in any bullshit in my past, Roland wasn't getting that grace from me. There were some things you didn't do to your brother or teammate. We didn't have to be close for certain lines to remain uncrossed. That nigga obliterated that line and I wanted nothing to do with him, no matter the price.

"Bruh, I hope August didn't make us come out here for nothing. After pulling that on you, I don't know." Nick rubbed the top of his head.

Izak sucked his teeth. "Glad we got to link up, though. It's been a while."

"True." I nodded, finishing my beer.

AUGUST SCHEDULED a formal meeting at the office to run her idea by me, Izak, and Nick. Once seated and ready, all she did was wear that silly ass smile. Whatever idea she came up with must've been a no-brainer.

"Sis, you gon' sit there or you got something we can smile about too?" Nick gestured at the three of us, leaving out August's assistant, who sat at the end of the long conference table. "What's the big news?"

"Eek! I came up with something that will give all your burnt out asses something to do with your time. Eventually, the money will come. For now—"

Izak leaned forward, pushing his clasped hands closer to the middle of the table. "Hold up! This plan doesn't pay?" He sat back again. "Hell, naw, August. You're supposed to put money in our pockets, not waste our time."

August looked to me for some backup and got hella disappointed. I didn't back a horse without knowledge of a plan.

"If y'all shut the hell up for one second, I can get it out. Damn! Have faith in a sistah." She straightened her posture and rested her hands on the table. "Now, there will be some compensation. The real money comes after we put in some work." August leaned back wearing that grin again.

"Auggie, spit it out already," I told her.

After giving me the Ice Cube scowl, she cleared her throat. "So, Airen has been getting some attention from execs who want to put a show together. A few priceless moments in his past interviews gained some traction with popular YouTubers. Since the offer to work with Roland was basically a nonstarter, I pitched the idea of actual friends talking football. They liked it but aren't sold yet. With other shows out there, we have to be inventive." She pointed her pen in the air. "I got a plan for that."

"Wait, us?" Izak inquired, like it wasn't as clear as day. "Man, we cuss too much. They will bleep the shit out of every sentence."

"Facts," Nick added. "To be honest, I hated press conferences. The camera is not my thing. Shit, it's not any of our thing."

I sat back and let them shut her down for the three of us. Sometimes, I thought the stress August had at home threw her off her game. She raised her hand as if she needed permission to ask a question. Out of respect, Izak and Nick closed their mouths and gave her the floor.

"Thank you." August clasped her hands. "My first question is, who scheduled this meeting?"

"You," we answered. She was about to be on that bullshit.

Her head bobbed before she continued. "Who's responsible for finding lucrative opportunities for each one of you?"

"You, August." Izak rolled his eyes.

"Then why the fuck can't I get the respect that comes with that job? If I were a white man, would y'all have all this to say before I even get a word out?"

"Hell, yeah!" I made known. Race had nothing to do with me not wanting to be in front of a camera. Especially when my agent, who was also a good friend of mine, was aware of why.

"Shut up, Airen," she snapped at me. "Look, the three of y'all were beasts on the field, and you recognize fellow beasts and their prey. All I'm asking is if y'all would consider hosting a show together. It doesn't have to only be sports. Any topic is fair game. Y'all will have a decent amount of creative control."

Nick shrugged and sniffed. "Shit, on the real though, a nigga bored than a muthafucka. I got some business popping off, but nothing that'll let me talk my shit unapologetically."

"I'm with Nick. I ain't really doing shit. Money is good for now. If this pops off and presents another stream, at least I'll be doing it with my brothers. But this nigga wants to live under a rock and shit. How's that supposed to work?" Izak pointed at me as they all turned my direction.

I didn't say a word. It sounded cool, but I wasn't trying to have my name out there again. No one wrote stories that fucked up my real world anymore. No tabloids. No gossip bullshit.

"Now, I'd love to say there won't be cameras. That is the end goal. You can't hide forever, Airen." August tilted her head to the side, failing her attempt to sucker me. "Think of it as a positive platform for the future when you want to get funding for the rec center. You'll need to get into people's pockets. What better way than to have a top show where you can discuss whatever you deem necessary?"

After telling Unc my idea, he convinced me to inform August. I trusted her and wanted her by my side if I went through with it. She'd know who I'd need to talk to and would provide me with the contacts.

We'd discussed plausible scenarios and weighed them against my desire for privacy. I wanted to do everything in the background, yet she argued my name could positively contribute to momentum. I was still deciding. I already had Nick and Izak's support.

The guys were now making the same stupid face as Auggie. "Man, I'll think about it."

"That's good enough for me." Izak clapped his hands once and stood. "I'm hungry. We can talk more about this over food. We'll get Airen to come around."

FIVE

Khaliyah

AUNT MAYA'S party was in full swing. I was over it already. The only good thing about it was my cousins and their kids. Until one couple at a time trickled out and left their kids behind. They weren't slick. Those punks planned this.

Uncle Rochon's friends were still a houseful downstairs. I helped set up everything before it started. My cousins chilled for a good thirty minutes before they dipped, childless. Babysitting duty for me, I guess. At least, it served as my excuse to stay upstairs with the kids.

Before we moved in, the game room was just another living room. My kids had transformed it to their liking. They had three gaming systems.

Uncle Rochon's great-niece got dropped off nearly the same way as the rest of them. My aunt showed her where the kids played and left her with them. I introduced myself and let her know where I'd be if she needed me. She had to be the same age as Aubrey, even though she was maybe an inch taller. The two of them played with Aubrey's stuffed animals when I left them.

I hopped on my bed to read but couldn't focus, so I put on *227*. I kept my door slightly ajar, since the boys were always loud when playing video games. With the music playing downstairs, there was really no escaping the noise either way.

Halfway through Sandra Clark's hilarious performance, Christian texted he wouldn't be able to pick the kids up next weekend. It was his last chance before school started. Two weekends a month turned into one, then it was excuse after excuse. This was his M.O. before we moved. I ignored the message and focused back on my show.

After the episode finished, a light knock came at my door. It couldn't have been one of my kids with their heavy-handed asses. I got up and opened it all the way to find the great-niece on the other side.

"Can I watch your TV? It's too loud in there." The way this little girl dipped her chin and twiddled her little fingers, many people fell for her cuteness. Her confidence in her adorability revealed itself. I bet she got what she wanted more often than not.

"Sure, you can." I pat the bed for her to hop up before handing her the remote. "You need help using it?"

"No. My daddy always let me choose."

"Well, okay then. Do you need anything to eat or drink?"

She nodded, and I realized I had completely forgotten her name. "What's your name again?"

"Ariyah Landry."

"Such a beautiful name for an even more beautiful girl." She turned on a smile that could melt the coldest of hearts. Including mine. I forgot what irritated me before she entered my room. "Let's get something to eat."

We left the room and passed through the crowd of kids. I asked if they wanted anything; no one did. So, Ariyah and I joined everyone downstairs.

Aunt Maya had a plate in her hand, heading toward us. "Look at my gorgeous young queens!"

I glanced at Ariyah, who still held my hand, blushing away.

"We're only coming for the food. I see y'all about to really tear it up soon." I nodded toward the band, setting up a keyboard, djembe drum, and a bass guitar.

"Rochon's buddies want to play for us since they'd just come from a gig. It won't be loud."

"Hey, this is your house. I wasn't complaining." I raised my hand, the one Ariyah still had hostage. "We're gonna get some food and eat upstairs."

"Sounds good. Everything that's spicy is labeled. Take care of baby girl. Her dad is super protective."

"And he left her here with y'all?" I giggled when she burst out laughing and gently popped my arm.

"Hush up." Auntie walked off and handed the plate to one of her friends.

Ariyah pointed to what she wanted, and after I made our plates, she followed me upstairs to my bedroom's balcony where we ate quietly for the first few minutes. I felt a little awkward babysitting a stranger's kid. That same kid ate with one hand and held onto my free hand with the other.

I finally broke our silence to ask her age and learned that the five-year-old wasn't in school yet. She explained her dad teaches her things and makes her watch shows like *Story Bots* and *Octonauts*. Apparently, her school starts next week while my kids just finished their first week.

Ariyah told me her mom was in heaven, so her dad was the only parent she had. She visited her Uncle Rochon a lot, but had never seen us here before.

Like I was conversing with an adult, I told her we moved here and were building a house. I gave her the rundown of who my kids were and told her we'd be living with my aunt for a couple more weeks.

After I cleaned up, we sat on my bed, watching *Abominable*. After a while, I laid down, and once she saw me, she did the same. Aubrey came in when she grew tired of the loud kids. The three of us had some girl time away from everyone. We played cards, then Candy Land twice. The girls really hit it off. They continued to play cards without me. I watched Aubrey teach Ariyah how to play war. She loved it. They were a comical little pair. I leaned back on the headboard and rested my eyes, listening to them talk and laugh.

A MAN'S voice made me jump. I looked around with one eye in case I was dreaming. Aubrey had left. A different movie played while Ariyah's head rested on my stomach.

When I glanced at the door, I thought I saw someone. I immediately brushed it off. A slight knock at the door brought my attention back to it. I almost jumped out of my skin when I saw a fuzzy figure move.

I blinked a few times and realized the man was real. He stepped a little closer and whispered, "I didn't mean to scare you. I'm Ariyah's dad."

"Oh." I looked at my watch. We'd been sleeping for over an hour. "I didn't realize we dozed off."

The man in the baseball cap slid his hands into his pockets. "It's cool. I wasn't trying to come into your space. I wanted to check in on her."

I glanced at the sleeping beauty. "She's fine. Such a sweet girl."

"Yeah, she is."

I rubbed her back softly to wake her up. Ariyah turned her face toward me and smiled that same heart-melting smile as before. I thumbed her cheek. "Hey, boo. Look who's here?"

Ariyah turned around and found her freaking twin from the features visible. "Daddy!"

Baby girl hopped up to hug her dad, kissed his cheek, then got back in bed with me. I couldn't help but laugh.

"That's all I get? You meet someone new and dump your old man?" he playfully asked.

Ariyah cheesed something special before she hugged me. "I don't want to leave Miss Khaliyah. Can you come home with us?"

"Um...I have to stay here. I'm sure I will see you again," I answered her the best I could.

Ariyah's head leaned to the side with a confusion that tugged at my heart. "But I like you. I want you to be my new mommy."

Her father cleared his throat and dropped his head. "Ari, it doesn't work that way." His eyes came up to meet mine. "I am so sorry, Khaliyah. Right?"

I nodded. "Right. It's okay."

"Go see if Aunt Maya has any more cookies," he told her.

"Cookies?!" Ariyah got out of bed and took my hand, leading me out of the room.

The little girl was not letting me out of her sight. We passed her dad, who'd now pressed his lips together. I could tell her question embarrassed him. I nodded subtly to reassure him it was okay.

Once downstairs, my kids had plates full of desserts. We must've slept hard. Aunt Maya picked Ariyah up and spun her around. "I saved you some cookies!"

When we finally separated, the energy changed. Her father stood next to me as if he wanted to say something. My body said some things that had to stay private. I chalked it up to my unofficially declared, yet very much felt, celibacy.

"We had a good time. Ariyah told me about her mom. So, it's understandable that she attached to me the way she did."

"I'm glad that she liked you at all. Usually, she'd only go to me, my uncle, or Maya."

"The two of them have been waiting for our introduction."

"Yeah, I've gotten the same push." He offered me his hand. "I'm Airen, by the way."

I took his hand and instantly felt warm. Not the tingles that lead straight to my panties. I became warm all over. It reminded me of *The Preacher's Wife* when everyone touched Denzel's hand.

Taking my hand back and ignoring what happened, I responded, "It's nice to finally meet you."

"Same."

SIX

Airen

I PULLED up to Uncle Rochon's house and could barely find a spot. I parked down the street and walked. He told me it was a *"little"* get-together, but this had Thanksgiving crowd vibes. The type that had me heading home before too many people trickled in.

After our first year in Houston, I became familiar with many of Unc's people. They were cool and didn't make me feel uncomfortable. I understood my face used to be on TV screens and magazines, but I'd rather people treat me like everybody else. If plastic surgery was a sane option, I probably would've done it.

Luckily, I'd been able to keep a very low profile. Growing my beard and hair out and never leaving the house without a hoodie or hat on worked for the most part. My cars were blacked out. I avoided most of my neighbors and did every other thing I could think of to stay out of sight.

Someone mentioned my name every so often on sports analysis shows if a player reminded anyone of me. Soon after those mentions, the sportscasters wonder what happened to me. I'd always dread the day when they'd have an answer to that question. For now, I had the privacy I'd wanted.

Praise God that He gave me a family that no longer milked

me dry. I learned an extremely hard lesson during my time playing professionally. Now, I was grateful for normalcy with my uncle and his people.

Ariyah had been here for a couple of hours. She hadn't called me at all, which meant she was enjoying herself. My baby girl didn't have many friends yet. Just me and our family.

My neighbor, who was also my childhood friend from Arizona and a huge reason for me making the move, had kids close to Ariyah's age. I thought it was plenty, but they weren't always available when my daughter wanted to play. This part never crossed my mind when I imagined raising her on my own.

One day, I'd have to let people in so my daughter could have a normal life with friends she loved. As scary as it was, Ariyah had a couple of days left before she started school. Aunt Maya helped me find a good private school nearby. I was sure she'd make friends there.

I let myself into my uncle's place. They always left the door unlocked for any type of gathering. The music hit my ears, and the smell of love in the kitchen did the same to my stomach.

"Nephew! You made it!" Aunt Maya called out, walking toward me. "Lemme get you something to eat."

She was loud enough to get some attention. Then the collective "Heyyy" followed.

"Wuzzup, fam!" I waved and walked with the lady of the house toward the food. If this woman did nothing else, she was going to make sure I had a plate in my hand.

As Aunt Maya plated my food, I searched the open space for Ariyah. "She's upstairs with the rest of the kids, boy. Your baby is safe."

She knew me too well. "Thank you. I know she's safe here. I get antsy with so many people."

"I know, boo. She's good. Your child attached herself to

my niece, and she is a mama bear. Ariyah is in excellent hands." She handed me the meal. "Eat first. Then you can go upstairs and find her. I bet she's not ready to leave."

"Thank you. I truly appreciate you and this, 'cause damn, this looks good."

"I try!" Aunt Maya winked, then left me to eat.

If only she knew how damn hungry I was after skipping lunch today. I cleaned my plate and still had room for more, but I needed to get eyes on Ariyah first.

I climbed the stairs after hugging a few people I hadn't seen in a while. Respectfully, they allowed me to stuff my face in peace earlier. That's why these were my type of folks.

The noise from the kids blocked out the noise from downstairs. Ariyah wasn't playing with anyone out here. I got one of Maya's grandkids' attention. "You know where Ariyah is?"

After a quick dap, her grandson said, "She's in there with Khaliyah."

I followed the direction he pointed. The door was cracked open, so I peeked inside to see what my baby was doing before interrupting her.

Ariyah was asleep, which would've instantly made me smile. My view of my daughter wasn't completely clear. There was a woman lying on her side with her knees bent toward Ariyah. Light snores came from both ladies. I reluctantly ignored the curvy woman's body and focused on getting my baby.

"Ariyah," I whispered loudly. No one moved. I cleared my throat and called her name again.

The woman stirred and slightly turned her head toward me. Maybe she was too tired when she looked at me because she rested her head again.

I called Ariyah one more time. The woman heard me and opened her eyes all the way. She looked up at me, almost doing a double-take.

"I didn't mean to scare you. I'm Ariyah's dad."

"Oh." She looked at her watch. "I didn't realize we dozed off."

"It's cool. I wasn't trying to come into your space. I wanted to check in on her."

"She's fine. Such a sweet girl."

"Yeah, she is."

UNC SNUCK UP on the side of me. He nudged me and said, "Don't look at her like that. You said you want nothing to do with a relationship."

"I'm only observing."

"Mmm-hmm. If not, we will need to have a talk first." He chuckled, patting my back. I assumed he meant to threaten me.

Aunt Maya did not play about her family. She acted the same way toward me since we met. It didn't take a long relationship for her to cover me. Being Rochon's nephew was enough. I loved that about her.

Unc excused himself, leaving me standing alone with my thoughts. I tried subtly watching Khaliyah. I'd be damned if it wasn't hard as fuck to look away. Her exterior was enough to pull any man's attention.

She was perfect. Her pooch gave away the sacrifice she made to bring children into this world. Many women had it, and unfortunately, they were ashamed of it. My late wife went under the knife to get rid of hers. It didn't matter to me. I witnessed the glory of her body changing to carry my seed and then birthing her naturally. It was beautiful.

Khaliyah, wearing sweatpants and a t-shirt, stole all of my attention. She gave off the vibes to leave her the fuck alone, which reminded me of myself. Now, I slightly understood why a person would risk it and ignore the obvious. If I actually believed in love anymore, I'd shoot my shot.

Khaliyah missed the line for height when God put her all together. Even in her petite frame, I couldn't stop staring. Her thick thighs sent my imagination to them wrapped around me.

Girlie had me tripping. Before anyone called me out, I started on my way to Ariyah. Halfway to where she sat at the bar, she'd already gotten Khaliyah's attention. I slowed my strides and watched her interact with my baby girl, bringing the most genuine smile to her face.

Khaliyah didn't seem annoyed about any of it. She stood there and listened, then moved toward the fridge. After grabbing something, she raised it up for Ariyah to see, and my daughter nodded, showing all her baby teeth. Khaliyah returned to Aryiah with a juice box. The special ones Maya bought were her favorite. She sat next to my baby with her plate of food and ate with her.

Why did that shit make me want to tear up?

Such an insignificant gesture explained why Ariyah asked her awkward ass question earlier. She liked Khaliyah because of the mommy vibes. I understood that, but she was wrong for putting us on the spot.

I TUCKED Ariyah in bed and kissed her forehead. She'd already picked her bedtime story and had it waiting at the foot of the bed. I grabbed it, ready to have her butt asleep in two minutes. By the way her eyes hung low and how quick her bath was, baby girl was beyond tired.

"Wait, Daddy." She placed her small hand on mine.

"What?"

"Do you think Miss Khaliyah is pretty?"

Oh, she's still on this?

I nodded. "All of God's creations are pretty. People, animals, and nature."

Ariyah pouted, not liking my answer. "Daddy! I mean pretty for a mommy."

"Not as pretty as my angel!" I jumped into her bed and tickled her until her eyes watered.

When she calmed down, she let me off the hook. I read the book and sang our bedtime song. The one my mom used to sing to me. Then she was off to slumberland.

Pretty for a mommy.

Khaliyah was gorgeous, but I kept that to myself.

SEVEN

Khaliyah

TIFFANY HADDISH's voice played in my head when we stepped foot inside the lounge Aunt Maya swore by. This was niiiiicccceeeee!!!

"How did you find this place, Auntie?" Karina asked Aunt Maya. "I thought I knew all the hot spots."

"Oh, baby, this is the best-kept secret. Some things are supposed to be advertised because they want any and everybody in their spot. This place is classy, and only a certain caliber of people are privy to it."

I moved closer to my aunt and whispered in her ear, "You know the owner, don't you?"

"Maybe I do." She winked and walked to the host's desk. He immediately recognized her and smiled.

"Welcome back, Mrs. Landry. Your section is ready for you," the man said as he waved his hand in the direction he wanted us to go. "Enjoy, ladies!" He watched us as the next handsome guy greeted us.

"Mrs. Landry!" he spoke with actual excitement.

"She must tip the hell out of them for this type of welcome," Karina whispered to me.

"Hello, William," Aunt Maya greeted him with a fist

bump. "How are things coming along here? Are you enjoying the work?"

"Yes, ma'am. I love it. Thank you again for the opportunity."

They walked and talked for about a minute as we strolled through the dining area. I was in love. From the decor to the vibes. It was both sophisticated and homey, if that made sense.

"Here you are! Laura will be your server today." William slightly bowed toward Laura, a young beautiful black woman with big, luscious curls.

We sat at the spacious booth in our cornered section, viewing the entire place. Laura took our drink orders and left a dessert menu at Auntie's request. Once she walked away, Karina and I stared at Aunt Maya until she folded. "Say what's on your mind or look elsewhere."

Neither of us said anything at first. Although the wheels were turning with a quickness.

I opened my mouth and eventually asked, "Did you leave something out all the times we talked about what we were into? Because something tells me you're doing the owner, or you are the owner."

Karina leaned over a bit and agreed. "I'm saying! I can see Rochon owning a place like this."

Auntie burst out laughing. "Maybe I have a little hand in ownership."

Our mouths dropped. "And you ain't say nothing? Oh, we are not family anymore. How could you keep this from us? This place is breathtaking!" I whisper-yelled.

"I live here, though." Karina crossed her arms over her chest and poked her lip out. "How could you have a whole grand opening and not invite me?"

"Or me? I would've been here too," I fussed. Laura dropped off our drinks, and we informed her we needed more time with the menu. Once alone again, all eyes were back on my aunt.

"Are y'all finished or are y'all done?" Aunt Maya asked with her shut-the-hell-up face. Karina sucked her teeth, and I rolled my eyes. "Now, I could've told you sooner, but I didn't. Forgive me. I like to see something become successful before sharing it with those closest to me. This place already had a grand opening before we hopped on the bandwagon. The owner needed help, and the place had great potential. We stepped in, invested, changed a few things, and this is the result."

After giving her the biggest pout face, I told Aunt Maya, "I'm proud of you. Would've loved to have known before now, but hey." I shrugged.

"I guess we're happy for you," Karina said, all stank, then laughed.

"I'm happy for you, too. I heard the jailbird done made it back to his nest?" Aunt Maya blurted after side-eyeing us hard.

"Khaliyah!" Karina's head swiveled my way with tight lips, waiting for an explanation.

After taking the longest, careful sip of my mimosa, I placed it down on our table and cleared my throat. "See, what had happened was..."

"I need to get new friends." Karina sat back in her seat. "Y'all too comfortable with my business."

"Girl, hush up and tell me what happened. We ain't friends anyway," my aunt said with no hesitation.

Karina clutched her imaginary pearls with genuine hurt in her eyes, even though she was playing.

Auntie leaned in to make her next words clear. "It's the truth. We are not your friends, little girl. We are your family. Both of y'all are like the smart-ass daughters I never had."

Karina and I locked eyes, then immediately nodded. We were definitely the daughters that would've gotten our asses popped every time we opened our mouths. Karina was truly like a sister, so Aunt Maya was right. Then again, my aunt felt more like a big sister/mom when she needed to be.

"Touché." Karina took a long sip of her mango mimosa. "Still, do we have to talk about him?"

I nudged her to share what went down. "Long story short..." Karina started. "I searched his apartment after I learned that the gifts he'd been giving me were stolen."

Aunt Maya's jaw almost hit the floor. "How the hell? Wait, how did you know they were stolen?"

"Khaliyah may have suggested it, and I obliged to prove her wrong," she admitted.

I sipped and listened while bouncing my leg for distraction. Trying to keep all of my feelings about it to myself. It took everything in me not to say those four words.

The waitress politely interrupted our conversation by placing another mimosa in front of me. "Oh, I didn't order this," I informed her.

The smile on her face made me nervous. "This is from the gentleman in the red shirt at the bar." She moved to the side so I could see him. He was fine, but young as hell. "He also gave me this."

She passed me a note.

You are incredibly beautiful, and I would love to talk to you. May I?

I pulled a pen from my purse and wrote on the other side.

I appreciate the compliment. I am divorced with three kids. So, no. I'm sorry. Thank you for the drink.

"You're never gonna find love again if you don't let it catch you," Aunt Maya said. I saw her peeking at my note.

"I never want love again. No need to lead a man on if I'm not interested."

"I tried, Auntie," Karina rolled her eyes. "This fool acts like Christian was all life had to offer, and she won't try again.

It's been over a year since the divorce, and years prior that they weren't really together, if we're keeping it real. Your niece is stubborn."

"We'll see about that." Aunt Maya pursed her lips.

"If God sees fit for me to love again, I'm not against it. I'd need to really trust the person with my heart. I chose Christian on my own, and look where it got me."

Auntie had a bit of sadness in her eyes. "I hear you. Just don't harden your heart because of that idiot. Keep healing and pray for what you want. I've known you all your life. You've always valued marriage, and you were so happy when you finally got into one. Unfortunately, it didn't turn out the way you intended, but I believe that it's all working according to God's plan for your life."

She must've noticed me stiffen a bit at that last part. Aunt Maya tilted her head down and made sure we made eye contact. "Khaliyah, if Gammy or I didn't teach you anything else, we taught you that all things work—"

"Together for my good," I finished. "Auntie, I swear I believe that. It will take some time to want what I used to want."

Karina stayed quiet. We've had these conversations throughout my divorce process and after. I've been apart from Christian for over two years now. There were no feelings there anymore. The failure of something so significant to me hurt more than the person I was no longer bound to.

Aunt Maya would probably understand more than anyone else. Uncle Rochon was her second husband, and they were perfect together. If that was what God had for me, I'd take it in a heartbeat. The problem was trusting my judgment if the opportunity came along. My kids were enough for me. If God says differently, I trust that he'd reveal that to me. As of now, love was not on the agenda.

EIGHT

Airen

"Kay, hold up. Shit," I got out through gritted teeth.

Khaliyah was sucking my soul through my dick. She seemed so quiet and innocent when we met, yet here she was, taking all of me down her deep throat.

I allowed my head to fall back as I enjoyed the hell out of her skills. All that ran through my mind was what I'd do to her next. When my head was up again, I glanced down at her because her energy suddenly morphed. It felt dark.

"Kay?...Kay?" I tried to get her attention when her body flattened.

All of her plush curves that I adored had disappeared right before my eyes. Her mouth even felt different on me.

I pulled her head up by her hair and saw the deep black, sinister eyes of Mercy. Her face had sunken in even more than I remembered. She cried tears of blood when I pushed her off me.

"Why wouldn't you save me, Airen? All you had to do was love me more. You could have saved me." She stood at the foot of the bed.

I froze in place, unable to speak a word, even though I fought like hell to. Mercy took one slow step after the other, scratching her inner elbow covered with needle scars. The closer she got, the *glossier her red eyes became. The white powder under her nose became visible.*

"All you had to do was love me enough to save me, Airen."

Her bony fingers inched closer to my face. I focused on her frail body. I cried at the sight of her ribs through the same lingerie Kay wore moments earlier.

I wanted to say that I loved her, but she chose the life she wanted over me. I wanted to say I was sorry. Nothing came out.

"You only see what you want to see. You're going to lose her too if you don't love her enough."

As if she read the look on my face, Mercy answered me by briefly transforming into Khaliyah. Kay's curves were slimmer this time, and she had a needle in her hand. Her hand moved closer to her arm, so she'd inject herself with whatever was in the syringe.

I tried my hardest to move, speak, even scream, but it wouldn't come out.

Kay stumbled back, and the needle broke into her skin. Before she tried to use her thumb to put enough pressure on the syringe, I broke free and dove toward her.

"NO!" I woke up to my voice. "The fuck?"

My clothes were drenched in sweat. I slept on top of the comforter. I didn't know how I got so hot. I must've fallen asleep on the sermon I tried to watch last night. The clock read three forty-eight a.m.

I'd been having crazy ass dreams about Khaliyah since I met her. It'd only been about us fucking or laying with each other, staring like we needed no words to communicate. It was all weird, but tonight was...I didn't even know what to say about it.

I removed my clothes and took a quick shower. I was still tired as hell, but my ass was not about to close my eyes after that dream. Instead, I turned on my laptop and researched dreams about ex-spouses.

Mercy's words played repeatedly in my head. The internet gave many opinions. Some sounded crazy as hell, while one explanation grabbed at me.

Guilt.

Khaliyah was an attractive woman with a body that made me want to give her anything. I wanted her. I interpreted my dreams about her as being lustful. Guilt with Mercy kind of cut me.

I didn't feel responsible for my wife's demise directly. Indirectly? That was a whole other story. My guilt came from giving her access to what my fame offered. I would've never guessed she'd get sucked in the way she did. She became addicted to that drug before her introduction to actual narcotics.

Why did she keep saying that I didn't love her enough?

I gave her everything I had. My only limitation was my time. I had a career that demanded more from me than she expected. I loved her more than she loved me. When she understood that, she took advantage of it. Once she got hooked on the fame *and* drugs, I pulled back. We had a daughter to take care of.

The sun crept into the sky before I tried to get some sleep. The moment I shut my eyes, Ariyah opened my bedroom door.

"Morning, Daddy," her somber voice spoke.

"Good morning, Ari. Whatchu doing up already?" Ari stood in front of me with her head hung low. "What's wrong, Angel?"

With her eyes still trained on the floor, she answered, "I had a bad dream." Her lips trembled, and her eyes watered.

"Awww, I'm sorry." I picked her up and placed her on the bed next to me. "Tell Daddy what happened. You know I can fight monsters from your dreams, right?"

She slightly giggled. I was happy to see her smile, even for a little. "No, you can't, Daddy. Only Jesus can."

"A'ight, maybe so. Did you call his name in your dream?"

The corner of her mouth raised her cheek. "I tried to, but I couldn't talk for some reasons."

I tried not to laugh. She always said, "for some reasons." I gave up on correcting her.

It clicked that we were both prohibited from talking. I'd be lying if I said that shit didn't scare me. I barely took on the attack. Ari was only five. Why the hell would it happen to her so soon?

"Mommy came in my dream," she shared.

"Sh-she did?"

Ari nodded as she faced me on the other pillow. I wiped her eyes before her tears fell. We were both on our sides at this point. My baby was scared.

Reluctantly, I asked, "Can you tell me what happened?"

"I was playing with Miss Khaliyah and Aubrey. We were having a tea party in a really big dollhouse. It was fun. Then the doorbell rang and Mommy came in."

As she recalled her dream, I prayed that clarity would come from last night. Both of us dreaming about Mercy couldn't be a coincidence. We'd been on our own without her for three years. This never happened before.

"Mommy looked sick. She tried to hurt Miss Khaliyah. I wanted to stop her, but I couldn't move. Aubrey jumped on Mommy, and Mommy hit her really hard. She fell on the floor like she was sleeping. I was crying and tried to scream for Mommy to stop, but I couldn't talk."

"I'm so sorry, Ari." I rubbed her arm, thinking of ways this related to the real world.

We both had dreams about the same people and had the same reaction. I didn't take shit like this lightly. I needed some type of answers so we'd both have some peace of mind.

My baby girl's tears gut-punched me. I hated to see her sad or hurt. One thing I failed to save her from was her dreams. I'd be damned if I didn't try.

"You wanna pray with me this morning?" I asked.

She nodded her head before sniffling. I kissed her forehead and cheek before drying her eyes again. We moved from our spots and positioned ourselves on our knees on the side of the bed. If I couldn't protect her physically, I'd go to God to protect her spiritually. If nothing else, this felt like a spiritual attack.

My job as a father didn't stop at providing for my daughter. I had to be and do more than live in the same house. I was my daughter's protector, provider, first love, leader, emotional guidance, spiritual teacher, and so much more.

I had to pick up the slack of a nurturer. That part didn't come easily. I learned a lot from the women in my life and from a few books. I didn't want to leave it to chance. I wanted to give Ariyah everything she needed with the resources I had. Tangible and intangible.

NINE

Khaliyah

GAMMY SENT me on a grocery run since she forgot some items for the fish fry tonight. I drove to the store I'd frequent once we move into our new house next week. Living with my aunt was cool since they had plenty of space, but I'm used to being the woman of the house. My closing was on Tuesday, and I couldn't be more ready. I felt like Norbit.

After grabbing a basket, I opened my notes app to check the list of items. We were spending the weekend with my grandparents since PopPop wanted to take Ashtyn fishing this morning. PopPop threw most of the fish back and only kept what we'd eat. It was his peace, and Ashtyn had grown to love it. Aydyn and Aubrey were not mentally made for nature. I blame myself with not an ounce of shame.

After getting the produce on the list, I made my way through a few aisles. It gives off the wrong vibes when I'm alone with no wedding ring and no kids. Every time without fail, the first thing out of my mouth if a man was bold enough to approach my perfectly purposely placed bitch face was "I got three kids." It worked wonders for me. Ain't nobody tryna play with these little boys in men bodies.

A man with the perfect height, the kind that can eliminate my need for a step stool, and a sexy ass walk, strolled through the aisles gathering groceries. I peeped him a few times but never made eye contact. His eyes were damn near covered, since his hat sat so low. But...dayum!

The energy oozing from that man gave me all the feels in all the right places. I was immediately pissed that I couldn't use any of my toys until we moved into the house. Dude was definitely suitable material to imagine, even without seeing his face.

I had one more aisle to go. Aubrey needed more allergy medicine. Right when I grabbed her preferred flavor, Mr. HeCanGetIt headed straight for me. Somebody needed to come and tell me why my knees tried to rat my ass out. I mean, he gave the weak-in-the-knees vibes, but I wasn't tryna do nothing for real. I prayed he didn't notice.

Shit, he probably would if he got too close. I read in a romance novel about this dude who could smell the girl's arousal through a fucking door. In case that shit was possible, I spun my basket around to leave before he reached me.

"Ay, Khaliyah. Right?" came from his lips.

The hell? He knew me? I didn't recognize him. He wasn't a forgettable figure by any means.

I slowly turned his way and saw a smile that turned the faucet on. Men who tried to be hard and not smile irked me. If you got nice teeth, show them suckers off.

"Who are you?" I asked, because I couldn't see much of his face.

He snickered with a huff. "I guess you wouldn't actually remember me."

As soon as he said it, I did. The similar smile and then the voice close up. Airen. I convinced myself to forget him the night we met. He seemed like the type that'll make you do things you'd regret but didn't care in the moment because you were with him. I didn't need that type of weakness in my life.

"I do. Can't say I remember your name. Forgive me." I lied.

"It's Airen." He narrowed his eyes in the sexiest damn way.

"Got it. I'll remember next time since we're basically family now."

"Nah, not really." He laughed before licking his lips.

See! He was one of those niggas who knew they could get the drawers. I didn't have time for it. I wanted it but no time to fall for that thang and then having to let go of it for good. Nope.

"Why you up in here with your hat so low? That's why I didn't recognize you. You looking like a creeper."

A fine ass one.

"I have reasons I don't want to be seen."

"Oh, okay. It's because women will throw their soaked panties at you."

Airen tilted his head with an unforgiving smirk. "Is that what you want to do?"

I said that shit out loud? There was no way to even play it off.

"No, you just look like that type of guy."

"Mmm."

The vibration of that small sound was bad for my impromptu celibacy. I needed to get my ass away from him. I'd never said aloud what I thought privately. Bad sign. He got my mind working against me.

"Where's your little beauty?" I asked to change my thoughts.

"She's actually with your aunt. She wanted to sleepover because she thought you and your daughter would be there."

My brows raised in regret. "Aww, that sucks. I wish we would've known. We're with my grandparents this weekend. Then I'll finally get the keys to my new place."

"I heard. Maya gave me the rundown. You're actually

moving into the same community I live in. It's massive, but we'll be neighbors."

"Shut up! Seriously?" My eyes bugged. He nodded. "Well, we can have a playdate in maybe a month. We're kind of starting over and will have to furnish the place."

"I have a fully furnished house. So, if you're down, we can host y'all. Plus, I have a game room I'm sure your sons will like."

"You know what? I think I'll take you up on that." I sealed the deal with a smile I prayed wasn't too obvious. A little time with him could fill my reel by the time I find my box of goodies.

"Let me know when you're free. You can text me. I'll give you my number. You got an iPhone."

"Eww. Never mind. Me and my Android will have to pass. I can't with you iPhone people."

Airen burst out laughing. "You ain't even gotta be like that. Just type in your number."

I playfully rolled my eyes. "Ugh, fine. But don't be turning your nose up at me."

Airen stepped a bit too close for comfort, but I played it cool. Well, I hoped I did. "Khaliyah, my nose will always be up around you." He looked down with eyes only to tease at our height difference.

I sucked my teeth and stepped back a few paces. "This is why I can't stand tall people. Always got jokes like any of us have a choice in the matter."

"I'm not that tall. To you, I might be since you're so—"

"Oop! You better not say it." We laughed. "Let me get out of this store, mister. You might try to insult me again."

"Never that, Shawty Doo Wop." He cracked himself up with that one.

My mouth fell open. "I'm done with you." I pushed my basket toward the nearest register.

Airen apologized but got side-eyed because he was still laughing. All I imagined was that episode when Martin thought he had a kid and the little boy wanted to keep his barbershop name. That was the only reason I laughed too.

I finished before he did. I only had two bags. When I got back on the road, I was already defeated. He was a goofball like me. Under that too damn sexy exterior, he was cool.

Christian lost his funny bone when he started working with his parents after college. I was suddenly immature to watch what I watched or to laugh at lighthearted or silly comedy. I lost the friend I thought I had for life.

Airen may be a new one minus the for life part.

TEN

Airen

AFTER PUTTING MY GROCERIES AWAY, I went to pick up my princess from my uncle's house. The time alone gave me space to understand my thoughts. Processing things my way before I brought it to others usually worked, but this time had me worried.

Seeing this woman in the store after constantly seeing her in my mind threw me for a loop. Fear wouldn't get the best of me all because I didn't have a full understanding of my feelings. I prayed to God for wisdom, since nothing was clear.

I squeezed the steering wheel tighter every time I felt Khaliyah on me from my dream. The sensation was intense, which made our little run-in hard to endure. Something about her gripped me physically and mentally. At the same moment, I shook off the image of Mercy and the words she said to me.

Ever since that night, my thoughts recited, "You could have saved me if you loved me enough." I played every conversation and scenario I clearly remembered and in all of them, I gave Mercy what she wanted. Not including the last time we spoke.

What Mercy said about Khaliyah wasn't as big of a deal. I'd only seen her twice. Nothing would come from it. Although flirting with her was fun, relationships were not in play for me. Khaliyah had already been someone's wife. That only meant she'd be searching for something better or she'd remove herself as anyone's prospect as I have.

I couldn't have anything casual with a woman related to Maya. Her body tempted me, which explained the dreams. They hadn't stopped. I wished the first one would've been it. Each one afterward was the two of us hanging with our daughters. Nothing sexual, but we felt familiar with each other.

Ariyah dreaming of Khaliyah and Mercy the same night I did made me curious. Why would we both fantasize about the same woman? Ariyah wanted a mother figure, so that was crystal. My brief yearning for a taste of her shouldn't have been enough for her to invade my dreams. However, she moved in like I'd given her an invitation.

If she persistently dwelled in my thoughts and dreams or my daughter's, I'd at least learn more about her. Maybe we had business to attend to that neither of us was aware of. Sometimes, connections were opportunities outside of romantic relationships.

I found Maya and Ari on the patio after Uncle Rochon let me in. "Daddy!" Ari hopped down from the outdoor dining table and darted straight for my opened arms.

Unc reclaimed his seat before I sat next to him with Ari in my lap. My daughter's mouth ran a hundred miles a minute as she shared every detail of the last two days with her great-aunt and uncle. She even reminded me that Khaliyah wasn't here the entire time. She said it so dramatically and bummed out; yet she had a great time.

Once the rundown ended, Ari continued coloring. She sang along with Jonathan McReynolds' music playing on the TV.

Maya had a look on her face, and I couldn't figure out

why. When I glanced at Unc for a clue, his expression was the same—a half grin and a raised brow.

"What happened?" I asked. "Why y'all looking like that?"

The two of them met eyes and giggled. What the hell was up?

Maya cleared her throat and stretched her hands out over the table. The smile on her face relieved some of the worry.

"We had an interesting conversation today." She motioned between herself and Ariyah.

I leaned my head slightly to the side. "About?"

"Come with me inside. Help me get us something to drink. You want water or apple juice, RiRi?" she asked Ariyah.

"Water, please." Ariyah never broke her concentration on her picture.

Maya waved for me to follow her. Once we reached the kitchen, it came out. "Do you talk to RiRi about Khaliyah?"

My head jerked back, almost offended by the question. I also didn't want to make it obvious how much I'd been thinking about Khaliyah. Playing things off with Maya never worked out for me in the past. The woman read minds and no one could tell me differently. I tried to block the thought so she wouldn't sense it.

"No. Why would I? We only met one time." *Twice.*

"So, you're telling me you haven't thought about her since? Your daughter is pretty invested in trying to spend time with her. I figured y'all talked about her."

"Maya, all she said was that she wanted to play with her daughter." I sat down. Maya would read too much into this and then I'd do the same. More than I already had.

"So, she never mentioned she wanted you to marry Khaliyah?"

I burst out laughing. "Come on now. Ari is a little lonely. She saw a woman with a kid her age and thought that was the best way to play with the little girl every day."

"Hmph! I got a different explanation." Maya pulled a wine glass and small hard plastic cup from different upper cabinets. She grabbed a bottle of wine from the wine fridge and poured herself some.

"Look, she's only five. She wants a female figure in the house with her all the time. Khaliyah is the first woman she knew wasn't an employee or relative of mine."

"You got an answer for everything. Can you explain why she said an angel told her she'd meet her new mommy the day you both met Khaliyah? Or why she's planning to make you two like each other so you can be happy, too?"

My eyes shot straight to the floor. For a moment, I looked up at Maya, checking her reaction. Her face was still, but held a smirk. Not wanting any more time to pass, I asked, "She said all that?"

"And more. Ariyah is pretty damn convinced and there is something about little ones having that much conviction about anything." Maya drank some of her wine.

"Yeah, but I'm not tryna find a wife or date. I'm good with it only being the two of us."

Maya rested her right hand on her hip after placing her glass on the counter. "Is she?"

Nothing made sense, yet it all kinda did. I hadn't processed any of it enough or with the wisdom I'd requested to be sure. "Even if she wasn't, I don't have to marry some random stranger because of it."

I knew little about Khaliyah. Those words exiting my mouth felt like a jab toward her, and I didn't like it. She was a complete stranger playing what ifs with my mind. I settled on raising my daughter alone. Two brief encounters with a woman wouldn't change that. How crazy or desperate would I be to think otherwise?

"No, you don't. I'm only saying you should be open to the possibility for both of y'all's sake. Khaliyah would be a pretty damn perfect catch if you ask me. I damn near helped raise her, so she has the ultimate stamp of approval. The body, the face, the heart. All top-grade."

"Really, Maya?"

The woman shrugged with way too much confidence in her words about her niece. "What? I'm serious. If y'all were a couple..." she drifted off somewhere else with a smile across her lips. "Ahh. I see it now. The wedding. RiRi having siblings and a family she deserves."

"I am the family she deserves." I tried not to come off defensive. Everyone assumed that being a single dad was a bad thing.

"You are. She needs you. You both have been through an ordeal. Obviously, she hadn't witnessed or experienced as much of it as you have. Mercy put you through it. Trust me, I know."

"I wasn't blameless. If I had done more, maybe—"

"Aht. Unh-unh. You will not blame yourself. We've been through this." Maya placed her hand on my shoulder. "She was very much an adult responsible for her own actions, Airen. Do you hear me?"

"I do." Mercy's words got to me again. "None of this was part of the plan. We shouldn't even be having this conversation. If shit didn't fall apart, I'd probably still be playing ball with a wife and a few kids back in Arizona right now."

"Boy, let that go. What was the first thing I told you after all of this came crashing down?"

I rolled my eyes, not wanting to admit that I'd consistently, conveniently, forgotten Aunt Maya's favorite scripture. She'd tell me whenever I'd lose sight of things when plans failed. I shrugged and mumbled my answer.

Maya held her hand to her ear. "Hmm? I'm sorry, I didn't hear you. You need help?" With her hand on her hip, whenever she knew she was right, she started, "You can make many plans..." she waited for me.

"But the Lord's purpose will prevail," I spoke up, finishing what I should meditate on.

"That's right. Etch it in your heart, Airen. God's purpose will prevail every time in every situation. It will all make sense in due time." She placed her hand on my forearm. "Now, listen to me. I don't want you to hold every woman accountable for Mercy's actions. Only for their own. Don't assume all women are the same."

Maya stopped and laughed at the ceiling. "I told Khaliyah the same thing days ago. Y'all seem to think because you had horrible experiences the first time around with nuptials that it's not worth trying again. Real love exists. Look at me and your uncle. What if we felt like giving up on finding the real thing after being burned by the frauds?"

"Then you wouldn't be lecturing me right now," I barely mumbled.

"Forget you, little boy." Maya pushed my forehead. "I'm trying to teach you something. But go ahead and be stubborn. You'll regret it one day. Trust."

The patio door opened. "What happened to my water?" came from around the corner. When Ariyah peeked her head in the kitchen, she giggled at Maya's face. Maya bared all her teeth because she'd forgotten all about it after getting the cup.

"Auntie sorry. Your daddy was being hardheaded, and I had to tell him about himself."

"You got in trouble, Daddy?" Ari's concern was adorable. With everything that we'd experienced the last two plus years, I loved the way she loved me. It was without reason in my head. I was her father, and that was all it took. If only love always worked that way.

I gestured the amount of trouble with my thumb and index finger. "A little."

Maya handed Ariyah a cup of cold water once I sat her on the countertop. She quenched her thirst before wiping her mouth with the back of her hand.

Ari looked at me with a straight face. "Can I spend the night again when Miss Khaliyah and Aubrey come back?"

Maya faked a cough to remind me of her warning. Little did she know, I'd made plans with her niece. I kept that piece of information to myself for the duration of our visit. I'd tell Ariyah whenever Khaliyah and I choose a date.

I understood where Maya came from, but if anything happened with Khaliyah, it had to be organic. For now, we could be friends who have daughters the same age. As they play together, we could learn more about each other. That was more than enough for now.

ELEVEN

Khaliyah

"Welcome home!" I told my babies as we walked through the garage door.

Each ran through the house trying to out-echo the other. I set my keys and our bags of food on the oversized island that first drew me to this floor plan.

"God, I thank you," I prayed as I removed our food from the bags.

The keys had been in my possession for a few hours. I waited at my aunt's while the kids were in school. This moment was one I wanted to share. The four of us stepping into our new home and future together.

I did this on my own. My track record of doubting my abilities to earn enough money to take care of my family was awful. Having a husband who despised you for the decisions you made for the benefit of your children slowly killed my confidence. I rarely recognized myself in that marriage. Although I stood behind certain unfavorable choices, I paid the price emotionally. My kids were still better for it. That was all that mattered.

Christian never knew how much I made with my "little hobby," as he called it. He felt my pennies were what I deserved after letting him down. The man also promised that pennies were all I'd be left with. The judge said otherwise. Yet, I'm almost to where his child support payments can go into a trust for the kids. I'd make enough next year.

For all of my troubles, I looked up to my high ass ceiling and whispered to both my spiritual enemy and the main person he used the most in my life, "Fuck you, nigga."

"Come eat!" I yelled toward the catwalk since the kids disappeared upstairs. As soon as the words left my mouth, the sound of rushing footsteps filled the house. "Stop running!"

All the noise halted. They came down like they had sense. Ashtyn let Aubrey down from his back and onto the island. I pushed their respective containers to each of them. Ashtyn blessed the food, and we dug in.

I scheduled the movers for tomorrow morning. The kids needed to be out of the way. Gammy would meet me here and wait for our new furniture to arrive. If everyone came on time, our bedroom sets, couches for the living room and game room, my new desk for my office, and TVs would be set up before I arrived from the storage unit with the movers. It'd be busy, but we'd get it all done in one day.

IT'D BEEN ALMOST a week in our home. Many unpacked boxes cluttered most rooms. We only opened what we needed daily. I was busy working since the holiday season inched its way closer. My clients' stores had to be ready. I prepared templates months in advance because I hated scrambling at the last minute.

My phone chirped as soon as I took a break from work and cut open a kitchen-labeled box. I checked my watch and saw a text notification from Fee-fi-fo-fum. I hated to admit that I'd been waiting for this man to use my number.

Since the night of our grocery store run-in, I checked my

phone a hundred and one times to see if he tried to reach me. I felt crazy to even think that he would. The shit pissed me off because I opened myself up for a letdown. That's when I had to admit to myself that I was intrigued.

A teensy bit.

Aunt Maya asked what I thought of him, and I lied. Before, when she asked me about a guy who showed me attention, I quickly blew it off. No one interested me because I had real shit to focus on. My kids were my top priority. Business was second. My sanity was third. It should be higher on the list, but I managed well in the chaos.

I still had to deal with their father. Communicating with him always made me hate men for a few hours afterward. No, they weren't all the same. I just wasn't in the business to give a damn either way at this point.

Fee-fi-fo-fum: Are you busy?

I got my phone from the office since I couldn't text what I wanted from my watch.

Me: Why?

Fee-fi-fo-fum: Who asks why? Yes or no would suffice Shawty Doo Wop

Me: Wow! I see you choosing violence today

Fee-fi-fo-fum: 😂😂

Fee-fi-fo-fum: Can you talk?

Instead of responding, I called him. It was my way of keeping myself in check.

Okay, it was possibly about being in control.

I didn't want to wait in anticipation of the man's call, even for a second. It'd help suppress any immature emotions.

"Yes," I said once it stopped ringing.

His laugh was distant. "That's the new hello, I guess."

"Do you have me on speaker?"

"Yes, but I'm home alone."

"Mmm-hmm."

"I am. You can trust me, Khaliyah."

Although he only meant I could trust he was alone, something told me I could trust him with any and everything. I had no plans to test that theory.

"Is there something you need, Mr. Landry?"

Airen laughed again. "Are you having a good day?"

"What?"

"It's not a trick question, Khaliyah."

Can you stop saying my name? It sounded too damn good coming from your lips.

"Yes, I am. Got a lot done. Still unpacking."

"A birdie told me you officially moved in last week. Congrats!" he voiced enthusiastically.

"Who's telling all my business?"

I allowed the wall to catch me. Multitasking while talking to him proved impossible. I imagined every facial expression. Unfortunately, I memorized his features when he spoke and laughed during our minimal encounters.

"The same couple who tell mine."

We shared a laugh. I learned little about Airen before and after we met. He was simply Rochon's nephew. Now, he had a face and a name to match.

"True." I nodded and smiled, grateful he couldn't see me. "Thank you. Everything went smoothly."

"Good. I'm here if you need anything. We are neighbors now."

"Oh, yeah! You did say you lived over here." I hoped I was more convincing than it sounded in my head. I never forgot that fact.

"You ever thought about when it'd be a good day for the playdate? Ari has been asking multiple times a day since I mentioned we agreed to it."

I imagined her cute little face with puppy dog eyes. "She's so sweet. Honestly, we can do it this weekend if you want."

"I do." Rushed through my speaker. I heard him exhale before continuing. "I mean, we do. Ari will be so excited. Saturday morning works for me. Maybe around eleven."

"It's a date. Play, I mean." *Khaliyah, calm your behind down.* "Playdate," as if he'd think otherwise.

A soft chuckle from him embarrassed me even more. "I gotchu."

Airen described where he lived, and I instantly became jealous. I'd passed by his gated section many times, wondering what the hell those people did for a living. If I paid what I paid, what were they paying?

I'd need to give my name to a guard at the gate to gain entry.

Who the hell was this man?

TWELVE

Airen

AUGUST, her family, and some employees came over this afternoon. It was her office's Wednesday off, which happened every two weeks. Since we were young, she'd been like an annoying ass know-it-all little sister. Her family was my family. When she called about needing my pool since her pool's pump broke at the last minute, I agreed.

The number of people I had to learn to trust became easier and easier. NDAs helped as well. One of the employees attending was August's actual family: her younger cousin, Khanan. Plus his friend, Tyree. August took them under her wing once they moved here with a business venture. Neither was an agent, but they wanted to fully develop a startup assistance company for new business owners. Both were still learning the ropes and doing a hell of a job.

Khanan worked with me over the past week to develop a proposal for my rec center. He admitted that my project was the first he'd ever had to assemble, but he took on the challenge. Khanan and Tyree were a great addition to August's team for pro athletes who wanted to do more than play their respective sports. Soon, they'd need more people under them. I told Auggie she'd have a new department and services to offer if this succeeded. I believed in those two young men.

We played in the pool for a while. Auggie's husband, Matt, picked up a ton of food from Oliver's Grill. Victor, my neighbor and lifelong friend, came over with his family. It was a lot of them. He and his wife owned Oliver's Grill and other spots around Houston.

As we broke bread, I introduced Victor to Khanan and Tyree. Victor had a heart for black entrepreneurs, especially those who made it their life's work helping other business owners succeed. It was right up Victor's alley, so this connection could be the start of a promising mentorship.

Khanan knew of Victor's old firm in Arizona and admitted that he had inspired him to follow the route he was on. August's agency bringing them on was a unique opportunity he couldn't pass up. Tyree barely spoke. The man was shocked about our friendship.

By happenstance, August attended the same university as Victor and me. Sharing a course or two turned into a lifetime of making money together. We aimed to help as many people as possible by sharing our knowledge and experience. The more young athletes and business owners we could save from making the same mistakes we'd made or witnessed others make, the better.

I recognized it was ridiculous to do all this and stay to myself. However, small connections like the one these men made gave me more motivation to move forward in the right direction. I'd get there.

We finished eating, feeling satisfied, and were ready to play games. The women started talking shit and a game of dominoes made assholes out of the men because we killed them, slamming the bones every chance we got.

"I really don't like y'all," Auggie said before getting up from the table. I followed her inside to grab more beers for everybody.

"Don't be so sensitive. Your mouth shouldn't have written the check," I teased.

The glare she handed me almost made me apologize, but I stood my ground. August nodded slowly as we made it to the fridge. "I'm gonna ignore your ignorance because I have a serious question."

I stopped my hand from grabbing the beers and turned toward her. "What's up?"

"When's the wedding?" This fool had the nerve to ask me with a straight face.

Dropping my head back, I stared at the ceiling for a moment. Why did everybody have this woman on their minds with the nerve to let the thoughts come out of their mouths? It was bad enough that she lived what seemed like permanently in my mind. My eyes fell back down to August's peering orbs. "This is exactly why I don't tell you shit. You gotta blow it all out of proportion."

"Who's the sensitive one now?" She crossed her arms. I forgot about her hating that phrase.

My shoulders dropped, mostly disappointed in myself. I was the one who told her about boundaries and setting them. It slipped my mind in the moment of excited arrogance. "I'm sorry for calling you sensitive."

"I forgive you. Now, um... Who is this Khaliyah woman? She came out of nowhere, and now Ariyah asked if she could be her mommy?" Auggie pouted, looking stupid. "Your daughter literally said that in front of her?" She laughed but loved the gossip, especially when it was innocent and didn't hurt anyone. My friend needed some girlfriends. For now, I loved her enough to give her something to talk about other than work. Lately, we'd been all about business. This! This, although annoying as hell, was my favorite side of her.

I leaned back against the fridge and ducked my head a bit,

trying my best not to give away my feelings about it. "I ain't gonna lie. Ari threw us off with that one."

"Baby girl knows something you don't." August bounced her brows, then made a dumb ass duck face. "God be speaking through these innocent chirren. Sometimes it's the only way stubborn adults will hear him."

"The first time I see the woman? Me and God are straight. He would've told me at a more opportune, non-embarrassing time."

Auggie burst out laughing, causing me to chuckle a bit. "Boy, you don't know what God will do until he reveals it to you. However, Ariyah may have chosen for you since you won't do it yourself. You said she was breathtaking. I've never heard you describe a woman that way."

August had a way of making me regret being vulnerable with her sometimes. Being my only female friend, she'd see this through a different lens than the guys. I didn't talk to the guys about Khaliyah. They'd be on my ass about hitting that. Even the thought of them talking about her like a piece of meat irritated me.

"What the woman looks like means nothing. We're simply having a playdate for our daughters. That's it. When I hung up my cleats, I hung my heart right next to them."

"Ugh! I hate when you say that. You can't retire your heart, dummy. Especially when God has the last word."

"A word he ain't mentioned to me yet. I'm not going there with anyone else ever again. God knows it and so do you."

Matt and Khanan came into the kitchen to get more food and drinks, interrupting and thankfully ending our conversation. We chilled the rest of the night. Meanwhile, my thoughts sent all of my what-ifs to heaven.

"How's my favorite girl in the world?" I asked Ariyah when she got in the backseat.

She focused on buckling herself in before answering, "Good!"

"What did you learn?" was my next question, as it was every day since she began kindergarten.

Ariyah always had something to say. So, I'd commute back home while she shared all her day's highlights. There were a few kids in her class that she didn't like. It always cracked me up when her face scrunched up, recalling something they had done.

"Daddy, why do kids like to say bad words? I tell them it's bad, but they keep doing it." Her concern was sincere and adorable.

I couldn't tell her what I felt because she'd repeat it and offend her classmates and their parents. I kept my response simple. "Sometimes people have to learn right and wrong their own way. They probably haven't learned it's wrong from their family."

"Well, I am going to pray for them. We are not supposed to talk like that. I know God doesn't like it."

I chuckled at her matter-of-factness. She wasn't wrong. "Praying is a great idea."

Once I parked in the garage, she unbuckled her seatbelt. "Miss Khaliyah and Aubrey still coming tomorrow?"

My daughter kept my spirits up. Her impatience never wavered. "Ari, nothing's changed since you asked this morning. You will see Aubrey tomorrow."

"You will see Miss Khaliyah! She's so pretty."

On that note, I exited the car to open the back door. Baby girl got out and headed to the garage entry door. My baby was growing up and needed to learn that not every thought had to be shared. I prayed she wouldn't say anything else embarrassing tomorrow.

After Ariyah washed up and sat at the island for her snack, I sat next to her. Somehow, I had to find the right words to accomplish my point, but not discourage her from being honest about her feelings.

"I understand you're excited about tomorrow, but we have to talk about what is and what's not okay to say."

Ariyah took a bite of her granola bar and nodded. She mumbled "okay" from her full mouth.

I started with my first point, leaning more on the table before us. "Remember the dream you had about Khaliyah and Aubrey?"

"Yes," she barely got out.

I didn't want to remind her of the nightmare. However, ensuring she kept it to herself was worth the temporary discomfort. "Let's not talk to them about that, okay?"

Ariyah paused before taking her next bite. "But for why?"

I scooted closer, thinking of why, besides it being our business. "Sometimes dreams can mean things. We want to understand it before we share it."

Ariyah took a moment, mulling over what I'd explained. "What if Miss Khaliyah can understand it?"

Damn, this little girl was definitely my child. I guess God gave me a dose of my own medicine. "Can we keep it to ourselves for now? For me?"

"Okay, Daddy."

Why couldn't that have been her response in the first place?

THIRTEEN

Khaliyah

As scheduled, I pulled up at the gate to Airen's community and waited for the guard to acknowledge me. He poked his head out of the opening. "What's your name, and who are you here for?"

"I'm Khaliyah Luke, here for Airen—"

"Gotcha." The older man cut me off and nodded. "He's expecting you." The guard smirked and then buzzed me in.

I followed my GPS down many streets until we reached a huge cul-de-sac. The house at the end was hard to miss. I was gonna ask Airen who lived there once we got to his home. Much to my surprise, the GPS led me straight to the same house that looked like a millionaire occupied it.

"What the hell?" I said under my breath.

"Whoa!" Aubrey admired from the backseat as we pulled into the long ass driveway. "Mommy, is this really Ariyah's house?"

I pointed at my dashboard screen's "you have arrived" message. "According to the GPS, yes."

As we exited the car, the house's front door opened. We headed toward the tall figure in the doorway before he had time to come to us.

Airen shot me a smile that appealed to my lower parts. I

mentally shut my body's reaction down. This meeting was for our girls, not for me.

Airen's arms wrapped around me like this was something we did. The warm feeling from the first time our hands touched had all of my senses jumbled. The smell of his cologne, the soft roughness of his beard brushing against the side of my face, and the assumed strength of his muscles that rubbed against me as his arms performed the simplest act of an embrace. This was going to be a difficult few hours.

After finally releasing me, the man took Aubrey's hand and bowed before her like she was royalty. His simple gesture put the sweetest smile on her face. "Ariyah is so excited that you're here. She's still preparing her room and will be out in a minute. Come in." He waved toward the inside of his house, if you could call it that. A mini hotel or a bed-and-breakfast was more like it.

I thought Uncle Rochon's house was over the top with its tall frosted-barred doors and grand staircase. It had nothing on Airen's foyer. Curved staircases adorned each side of the entrance with a unique chandelier above a large round table that rested comfortably in the center.

"You like pink roses, I see," I joked, eyeing the massive bouquet in a gorgeous vase. I'd probably have the same thing in my foyer if it looked like this. Those were literally my favorite flowers, and I wasn't a flower type girl. Something about them was so beautiful and youthful.

Aubrey walked to the table to see the bouquet up close. "Mommy, it says your name." At five, my baby could spell and read on a second-grade level. With our unique names, I taught them all at an early age.

I glanced at Airen before joining Aubrey near the table. The card, in fact, had my name. And correctly spelled? "That damn Maya!" I murmured.

"Maya said you might like them," Airen spoke from the same spot near the door.

Did he hear me?

"I do. Thank you." My attempt to keep my skin from heating failed. Our playdate already had me giddy on the inside. "What else did she tell you?"

A door closed upstairs, which brought all three sets of eyes to the top of the stairs. "We'll talk about that later," Airen barely said.

Ariyah appeared from around the corner, and Aubrey smiled harder than Airen had made the ends of my mouth spread seconds earlier. The boys were Aubrey's only companions, besides the adults in our family who played with her. My baby needed friends her age, and from the looks of it, she'd found a little bestie.

Once baby girl carefully reached the bottom of the stairs, she darted to Aubrey, and they held each other like they hadn't seen each other in years. Ariyah released my daughter and gave me the same love. Her energy was warm and spread throughout my entire being. I loved her already.

"Are you hungry?" she asked me and Aubrey. "We have food!"

"Sure." I followed her lead as she grabbed my hand. Looking back at Airen, he smirked at his daughter taking over.

Through the foyer, we turned left to find the kitchen of my dreams. Don't get me wrong, my new kitchen was also one of my dreams, but it was the fit-in-my-current-budget version.

A quick once-over at this custom kitchen was all I got before Ariyah stopped us at the massive waterfall island. The spread was beyond my expectations. Recognizing the pattern from this family, I adjusted my expectations for future reference.

Ariyah gave us the rundown on the pre-cut sandwiches—some with ham, some with turkey, and the others with chicken. I clocked the small platter of veggies, another with fruit, and a stack of kettle chips. There were dips, juices, and even wine. Ariyah pointed out that the wine was only for the grown-ups.

I took a seat at the island after making a plate for Aubrey. Airen did the same for Ariyah. Those two sat at the table behind us as if on a lunch date with so much to catch up on. They discussed school before I stopped ear hustling.

I put one of each half sandwich on one plate, a spoonful of each spread on another, then filled the last with some fruit. I wasn't used to eating veggies like this, but they were lightly grilled and smelled like heaven. With sprinkles of seasoning on top, curiosity got the best of me. I took a few pieces of broccoli and cauliflower.

Biting the sandwich with no sauce was good on its own. The smoked ham was perfect, the chicken was still moist even with the thin slices, and the turkey had peppered edges. Then there was the sauce. I thought it was simply mayo and mustard, but nope. The moan from my belly reached my lips, and I suddenly remembered I wasn't alone.

"I know, right?" Airen caught me slowly becoming addicted. "I see you ain't scared to eat."

"Don't judge me." We laughed. "This is delicious. You made this?"

Airen swallowed his food before speaking. Already brownie points if they ever counted. "Nah, I got it from this barbecue joint that Unc and I frequent. A friend owns it."

"Oh, yeah. Which one? I'ma have to check them out."

"O.C. BBQ. Ever heard of it?"

"No, and I'm mad that I've been back in Houston for a minute and no one mentioned it. Anything smoked is my favorite."

"I might have to take you there myself. Gotta give you the

rundown on must-haves. Then again, we may have to go a lot because you can't really go wrong. They have a lot to try."

"Are you asking me out on a date, sir?"

Airen wiped his hands, possibly choosing his words carefully. I might have opened myself up to something I didn't even want. "Just two new friends sharing a meal that I will pay for only because that's who I am."

Whew! Good save, Airen.

Recalling his getup in the grocery store, I looked him square in the face and asked, "You going incog-negro again?"

That question pulled a gut laugh from him. I loved it when men bellowed out a laugh. It seemed like a comfort zone. It also permitted me to be just as boisterous if I wanted to. Christian said my laughs were inconsiderate. Being a goofy person who loved a good chuckle, that judgment was discouraging.

"I don't have to. Not there, at least. I get the hookup with a private entrance to pick up my food or even dine in."

A private room? My brow attempted to reach my hairline. "Who are you?" I had no choice but to ask.

Our eyes met as he seemed to hesitate with his answer. He held our connection and said, "If we continue this friendship long enough, you'll find out."

Tilting my head, wondering how to take his response, I honestly admitted, "I don't know if that's intriguing or intimidating."

His head shook quickly as his right hand rose a bit. "The former, I hope. I don't want to intimidate you. Ever. Just protecting my privacy."

"Oh, unh-unh." The mystery was interesting, yet the reason may be enough for me to keep my distance. "You better not be somebody famous."

Airen chuckled before crossing his arms. "Why not?"

"I like a low-key, get to mind my business type of lifestyle. I'm chill."

"You are very chill. I'll give you that. I also prefer to keep a low profile. So, I guess you have no worries."

"The jury is still out, since you didn't answer my question."

Airen opened his mouth to respond, but our little ones appeared at the island. "Can we play now?" Ariyah asked.

"That's the reason we came, isn't it?" I gave her a nod and a wink.

"How about I give you a tour?" Airen stood to await my answer. I dipped my chin once in agreement, and he cleared our plates.

We started in the backyard. All I learned was that Ariyah required our presence another day to swim in her pool. Then another day, her dad will barbecue. And another for an outside tea party. She basically planned a month of Saturdays.

Playdates meant getting to know Airen. I wasn't keen on making new friends these days. My kids and work were enough outside of my breaks to spend time with my aunt, Karina, and grandparents. I guess I had to add these two to my schedule.

FOURTEEN

Airen

AUGUST SCHEDULED an afternoon meeting to discuss our focus group critiques. She assembled a group of her employees and told them to be brutally honest. Nick and Izak joined us virtually in one of August's smaller conference rooms.

"The overall reaction of the two episodes was outstanding!" August clasped her hand in front of her mouth, covering her big ass smile. "The group said you all were hilarious and genuine. They loved each segment but one. The title was a bit brash, but the content was great."

"Bet I know which one," I blurted.

Nick laughed on the big screen. "Me too. Izak, you've been outvoted. We told you that 'get the fuck outta here' wouldn't fly."

Izak swiped his hand at the screen. "It flies with me. We're keeping it. We grown. You said no filters."

August nodded, bobbing her head. "True, but Izak, we still need to be tolerable. Eighty-three percent of the viewers mentioned your mouth. Especially about you saying nigga every five damn seconds."

"Nigga!" I said to Izak, trying to lighten the blow to his ego. We all saw it coming.

"Muhfuckas wanna act like they never heard a nigga be

real, fine. I'll reel it back. Maybe I won't say shit." Izak leaned back in his chair, dragging his fingers across his lips as if zipping them.

Auggie rolled her eyes. "Stop being so damn dramatic, Izak. I want you to be yourself, but try to be more..." She moved her hands in circular motions around each other. Then she said, "Professional."

"Professional?" He caught an attitude, almost questioning her audacity.

"Professional, muthafucka. Cuz muthafucking listeners ain't showing up to listen to Samuel L. muthafuckin' Jackson talk about sports."

Nick laughed. "That sounds entertaining, though."

August cut her eyes at him, and he pressed his lips together. No one wanted to be on her bad side. Especially when she started cussing.

"Y'all seem to think this is funny. How about y'all laugh your way off my screen and out of my office?" She turned toward me.

"I ain't even say nothing," I defended. "But we hear you. I'm sorry."

Izak sighed. "My bad, Auggie."

"Me, too," Nick added. "We'll keep it professional."

"Thank you." August tugged on her collar before looking at the sheets on the table in front of her. "Now, we will do another two episodes with these critiques in mind and see if we can get a higher score. The goal is to get sponsorships and even be picked up for TV. More money means more opportunities to do good for your community." August looked at me with the last line. "I get you want to stay off the screen, Airen, but it's time to man up for the sake of your goals. Your days of hiding are over."

I pursed my lips to the side, considering her words. I

refused to admit she had a point. One I knew would come sooner than later. Guess my time was up.

"Look, it won't be overnight, but you all are Super Bowl champions and have great chemistry because of your brotherhood. This can turn into something really special. Your love for the game doesn't have to be dismissed, all because your old asses got hurt." The three of us caused a ruckus after that comment.

Auggie shushed us before closing the blinds. She picked up the remote and threatened to cut them off and find other clients for this opportunity. Knowing the league wanted to put a fresh new show together, August snagged a producer to create one herself. My refusal sparked this idea for her, and she'd successfully pull it off with or without us. Her credible threat gave her the floor and our undivided attention again.

Another thirty minutes passed as we locked in recording dates and research days for topic discussions. August wanted to make sure we took this as seriously as she did. Her vision for us surpassed ours since part of the fun was talking ball with our boys. When the meeting ended, the woman acted like our show would change the world.

"You good on time?" August asked.

"Yeah, Aunt Maya finished with her client early and asked to get Ariyah. Something about ice cream after school."

"Of course she did. Your child is spoiled."

"True."

"So, Maya sent over some potential buildings for the rec center. I had Khanan and Tyree check them out before creating a top three list."

"Okay, sounds good."

"It does, but I ain't gonna lie. Some of these abandoned buildings are in some not-so-great spots. The potential is there, but they look run down from the outside."

I tried not to let that discourage me. The end game would be worth whatever we faced.

August continued, "With that being said, can you ask Victor for a vetted list of investors and donors? We talked about it a bit at your house the other day, but I hadn't followed up officially."

"Yeah, I'll get on that."

"Good. Our business is done." August sat across from me with her hands resting on the table. She stared at me like she'd asked a question and was waiting for my answer.

"What?" I asked.

"The playdate, fool! How'd it go?" she damn near yelled.

"It would be best to ask what's on your mind instead of assuming everyone has telepathy."

August rolled her eyes and huffed. "I want to know how things went with you and Khaliyah. Is that clear enough for you?"

"It's clear that you need to stay out of grown folks' business."

Her face had "I hate you" all over it.

She slightly smacked her hand on the table. "You were right about one thing. I need some female friends. You get on my nerves."

"Looked like you hit it off with Nina at my house," I recalled.

"Yeah, we exchanged numbers, but that's your friend's wife. She may have pitied me because of something you said."

"Oh, you stupid, stupid," was all I got out before the pen flew by my ear. "You missed. Now, stop being a toddler. Nina is cool people. Plus, she has sisters. You might find yourself a tribe."

"You might find yourself a wife," she threw back at me.

"How the hell we get there? A playdate, Auggie Boggie. Nothing more."

"Yeah, but I know you. Your face changes when you talk about her."

"You're seeing what you want to see."

"Sure, Airen. Please don't mess this up and compare her with anything or anyone from your past. She is a different person and if you play your cards right, you will have a different, even better result."

I stood up. "On that note. I'm out."

August hopped to her feet. "Fine. Check to see if Khanan came back before you leave."

"Will do."

We stopped at the closed door. August placed her hand on my forearm.

"Love you, Airen. I'm not trying to fuss at you. I respect your stance on your non-existent love life. However, from the outside looking in, you may receive another chance at the real thing. Yes, all because your daughter said so. I believe she knows in her heart what she keeps blurting. I pray you open your heart to new things and close the door on the old. I'm rooting for you, big brother."

"Thanks." I gave her a piece of a smile before walking out and heading in the opposite direction from where she went.

Everyone saw potential in me choosing to be in a relationship again. Nothing was wrong with their hopes, but my experience taught me something different.

Lately, the pain of that experience stung a little less when I thought of the same possibility as my family. Being with the right person could right all the wrongs in my mind about my past. It won't ever erase it, but it would probably ease the power of terrible memories.

Khaliyah lived rent-free in my head. I might as well see if there could be something between us. If there wasn't, at least it would release the idea from my people's minds.

Deep down, I hoped they were right.

FIFTEEN

Khaliyah

I WALKED into Ashtyn's room after checking in on Aydyn. Christian would pick them up soon. My son has had difficulty forgiving his father, and I couldn't blame him. We were all heartbroken by the divorce, but since I was part of the union that broke, I had more time to understand what was going on and process it. Our kids were the last in our little family unit to find out.

"You ready, boo?"

Ashtyn kissed his teeth, dragging his feet across the carpet. He placed a shirt in his bag. "No."

"You still mad at me?"

"No, Mom. I don't want to go. I don't want to deal with Dad. All he's gonna do is take us a few places, if that, take pictures, and win the best dad award in his mind."

I laughed at the visual. "Be nice."

"Why? He wasn't nice to you. You always say we have to give grace, but, Mom, I don't have much more to give. At least not to him."

"Son, he is your father. I know you're upset right now, but you have the power to change things. Sometimes, when dealing with certain people, they need a gentle nudge in the right direction."

"Ma, I don't understand. You tell me all the time that men are supposed to be responsible and they are accountable for their actions. But Dad is somehow an exception? How did you even marry him?"

There wasn't an answer to that question that would sound pleasing. The last thing I wanted to do was bash the man to his son, but his fuck ups are just too big to be ignored.

To be somewhat fair, I said, "Ash, I can't say I'm sorry enough for the choices I've made that got us here. We were young and started a family before we really got to know each other. It's sad but true. However, I don't regret having you and your brother and sister. If this experience came with getting you guys here, then it was worth it."

Ashtyn dropped his head. "Yeah, I guess. But why is it so easy for you to apologize for a situation you didn't put us in? He did."

"Baby, we were married to each other. We had children with each other. We made decisions together and separately that contributed to our current situation. That's okay. I learned many lessons so far, and I will do all I can to ensure you don't have to make the same mistakes."

"Why doesn't he do that, too? He never apologizes. He never takes responsibility. Why do we have to be so respectful if he doesn't respect us enough to say he was wrong and he messed up?"

Where the hell did this grown man come from? I had no words. I sat on his bed with no words to make this better.

"It's not fair for me to tell him how I feel when he's supposed to see it. If he loved me, he'd see me. He's a fraud, Ma. He only pretends to care when people are watching."

My eyes pooled because I thought I had more time to mask the bullshit with Christian. He was a damn fraud. He was a coward when it came to facing his actions. He was all of what Ashtyn said, and I can't hide it from them any longer.

I reached my arms out to my son. "Come here." He sat next to me, then rested his head on my shoulders. "You are completely right. None of it is fair. It sucks, and it's life. No one is perfect. We have to accept what it is or try to change what we have the power to change. But with other people, we can only say our piece and hope for the best. I think it's time that you say what you need to say to your father."

Ashtyn sucked his teeth. "Man, he ain't gonna listen. All he cares about is Kaitlyn and fronting for everyone like he's the greatest dad ever. I hate it when he does that. He thinks he does everything right. I've watched him. I've listened to him."

"I guess there's nothing else I can say. If you want the relationship to change, make your needs known. Otherwise, like you said, he's not gonna care enough to see how you feel."

"Or you can stop making me go with him."

"Stop acting like I'm forcing you on a stranger, boy."

"Might as well be. He doesn't know me, Ma. He still thinks I like Pokémon."

We shared a laugh, which we both desperately needed at that moment. My baby was growing up and his bullshit meter was up and running.

The doorbell ringing was expected, but it didn't annoy me any less. After almost a month of random phone calls, Christian finally came to see his kids.

"Hey, Khaliyah," he greeted me before inviting himself in. One glance at the open floor plan, he opened his stupid mouth and said, "Nice little place you got."

I let him make it with his petty ass. "Boys!" I yelled so they could get downstairs and lead this nigga out of my presence. His negative spirit was not welcome here. I prayed over my babies every time they had to go anywhere near this man and when they returned.

"Hi, Daddy!" Aubrey appeared from my bedroom. She

finished her bath and put on her pajamas for our movie night playdate.

"My princess!" He opened his arms so she could jump into them.

As much as I couldn't stand the sight of him, Aubrey loved her dad as she should. I prayed she'd never meet the asshole that interacted with me on most occasions.

"I wish you were coming with us. I'm gonna miss you, princess."

"Me too. Me and Mommy will have fun with Ariyah and Mr. Airen," Mini spilled the damn beans.

I cleared my throat. "Boys, hurry up. I thought y'all were ready."

"We're coming, Mom," Aydyn shouted back.

"Mr. Airen? Who's he, princess?" he asked our innocent, yet big-mouthed daughter.

Christian's eyes stayed on me for a good minute, but I kept my attention on my phone, pretending like I heard nothing. When he looked back at Aubrey, I put my finger to my mouth so my little girl would remember what we talked about.

"He's my friend's dad. I think he's Mommy's cousin."

That was off script and lies from the pits of hell. Ain't no way I'd have the thoughts that invaded my mind about a relative. However, she seemed a bit confused after our last conversation about it. Because Airen and I technically have an aunt and uncle married to each other, Aubrey assumed we were cousins. I corrected her, but the idea of her being somehow related to Ariyah in her mind kept her from accepting the correction.

"Cousin, huh?" Christian's eyes were on me again.

"He's my uncle Rochon's nephew. So, by marriage, yeah," I clarified, to make him stop talking. "His daughter is Aubrey's age."

"You sure he's not a kissing cousin?" Christian stood after letting Aubrey down. "I know you're lonely. Cousin or not."

"Don't play with me."

Ashtyn slowly stepped his way down the stairs, passed up his father, and stood near me. "What's up, Dad?" He said from the island, then set his bag down and filled his water bottle with ice.

Aydyn came down. "Hey, Dad!" He hugged Christian before joining his big brother in the kitchen.

Christian looked like he wanted to say something to Ashtyn when he kept his distance, but that was on him. I talked to my son about it; however, a conversation between him and Christian seemed far off. Ashtyn didn't want to go with his father this weekend, but Aydyn did. I had to bribe this boy to accompany his little brother.

"I don't get no love, son?" Christian asked, spreading his arms.

I hoped they wouldn't do this in front of me. One wrong word, and I'd put my ex-husband out. There had been no disrespect between the two, but understanding Ashtyn's feelings and experiencing the levels of insanity that his father frequented, this could all go left.

"I said what's up." Ashtyn's chest puffed up a little after swallowing his water.

The tone down in my son's throat warranted a word, but I gave him passes as a teen going through what he was going through. "Ash, make sure you turned everything off in your room, please," I told him with a look to warn him about his attitude without saying a word.

"Yes, ma'am." He took off with a quickness.

"You heard how he talked to me?" Christian asked me like I gave a damn about his feelings. My concern was solely about my son.

Me: Please don't fight with your dad. You can talk to him one-on-one this weekend. Your sister and brother will follow your lead. Lead responsibly.

Ashtyn: I won't. He started it.

"Yeah, he's going through things. Give him grace," I requested of their father.

Me: Be mindful...

Ashtyn: of my words and reactions. I know Mom. It's hard.

Christian rolled his eyes. "You and this grace. These boys will be soft and disrespectful with all the grace you hand out. They need discipline."

Me: I understand. Next time, you can stay home. Okay?

Ashtyn: Okay ma

Me: I love you

Ashtyn: Love you too

There were so many ways I could tear Christian's ass up right now. I needed to practice giving grace as well. He was too ignorant to understand why I granted so much of it.

"Christian, feel how you want." I clasped my hands to keep my mouth on godly things. *Whew, Lord, if you don't get this man out of my house, you're about to be mad at me. Please, help me.*

Ashtyn slowly came down the steps again. "Alright, boys, y'all be good for your dad, and he'd better be good for you." I cut my eyes at that fool, daring him to start up again.

"Love you, Mom," Aydyn said, hugging me before picking up his bag.

"Missing you already," Ashtyn said during our embrace.

"Be good. God sees all. He will let me know and what we agreed to ain't happening," I whispered while staring into his eyes with the most seriousness I could conjure. Under it all, I didn't care if they gave Christian a hard time. He deserved it, but I raised my kids to be respectful even when they didn't want to be.

Aubrey and I walked the guys out. I watched Ashtyn rush to the back seat when he was the undefeated champ for calling shotgun. Something in me was unsettled about forcing him to go, but he'd be okay, at least that's what I told myself.

The moment the door shut and locked, Aubrey dashed for her backpack. "Are you ready, Mommy?"

"Mini, let Mommy have a minute. I promise we'll see Ariyah soon enough."

"Okay." She put her bag of toys by the garage door and walked to the living room to watch TV.

I went to my room and plopped on my bed for a minute to clear my head and regain positive energy. This playdate didn't need my pouty face or attitude. Although I wasn't blessed with the hidden emotions trait, I'd do my best to keep everything in. The last thing I wanted to do was to have Airen get an earful of business that didn't belong to him.

Becoming friends with a man that fine needed to remain light. Inviting him in with the personal stuff wouldn't work in my favor. I could see him saying all the right words, agreeing with me, and helping me bash my ex. Then we'd know how we looked naked together. Then the awkwardness would creep in once we realized we had nothing deep in common, and we'd have to break the girls' friendship up.

I had it all figured out in my mind. I understood how ridiculous it sounded and kept it that way to keep me in line. I was sure to stay in my lane with Airen. Eventually, he'd trust me enough to let Ariyah stay with us a few hours, and he'd go about his business. Aubrey didn't go to sleepovers at anyone's house, but I'd gladly host them.

As I took my slow breaths, a text notification chirped. I reached over to the nightstand to get it.

Fee-fi-fo-fum: I'll order something since it's almost dinnertime. Only if you want me

Fee-fi-fo-fum: *want me to

I got comfortable on my back before responding.

Me: I do. I can pick it up on the way. I'm in the mood for either seafood or Mexican

Fee-fi-fo-fum: Now you know I'm not gonna make you pick up anything

Me: No. I didn't know that

My phone rang with a picture of Ariyah. I immediately remembered what he told me on the first playdate.

"Too much texting?" I asked.

"Yeah. I hope it's okay to call." His voice sounded unsure about his choice.

"It's cool."

"I was gonna say we can look at some menus when you get here. I have a book full."

"What?"

"Ariyah's old nanny wasn't the best cook. She tried, and Ariyah's blatant honesty made the lie in her interview pretty obvious. She was good at everything else. Especially organization. Hence, a binder full of local restaurants and menus. They are even divided by the type of cuisine."

"Wow. I might need a copy."

"It comes in handy when I don't want to cook."

"Which is probably never," I teased.

"Ha! I dabbles."

"Yeah, sure. We will be there in fifteen minutes."

"You need something waiting on you when you get here?"

Like what? Your naked body? I'd take that if we didn't have the girls.

"As long as you've got some wine. I'll be good."

"I gotchu. See you soon."

The knock on my door informed me I was taking too

much time in my room. Aubrey poked her head in after she cracked the door open. "Are you ready now, Mommy?"

I kept my eyes on the ceiling as I rolled them. "Yes, little miss. Let's go."

"Yay!" Aubrey jumped with the biggest smile.

SIXTEEN

Khaliyah

ARIYAH BEGGED us for another Saturday fun day. This time, the boys joined since I didn't want to leave them home alone. My aunt and uncle deserved a break from all the babysitting.

Despite those excuses, I wanted my sons to meet a good man. Seemingly. Airen and I talked about life, but nothing too deep. So, I used "good" lightly. Yet, he was being trusted with my entire family in his home.

Once we drove past security, I smiled at Ashtyn and Aydyn's reaction, similar to mine and Aubrey's, the first time we visited. "Man, her dad must make way more than Dad," Aydyn pointed out, admiring the house from his window as we parked in front of the garage doors.

"You'd better not say that once we are inside. It's rude," I told him.

"Dad's rude," Ashtyn said. "He wished he had a house like this. That's why he dumped us."

"Ashtyn!" I fussed.

"What?! Ma, you know it's true. All he cares about is his money," Ashtyn spoke truthfully. I didn't even fight him.

Airen met us outside as usual. Aubrey was the first to reach him, and he bowed as before. Aydyn offered his hand and gave Airen a firm handshake, like his grandfather had taught him. Bitter me wanted to point out that Christian taught them nothing about being a man besides going to work. Anything from a moral standpoint or simply manners as a man came from me or my family.

"Hello, sir. I'm Aydyn."

"I'm Airen. Nice to meet you."

Ashtyn was next, but the boy froze once he made eye contact with Airen. My eldest son narrowed his eyes at the man's face and then backed away with his orbs damn near about to burst from his head.

Ashtyn's mouth flew open as his eyes stayed on Airen. "You-You're Air...Airen Landry." This boy's hands flew to the top of his head, and his knees locked as they did whenever he was about to lose it.

I shook my head as both corners of my mouth rose. "Boy, what's wrong with you?"

Aydyn and Aubrey met eyes with me, and we all shrugged. Airen didn't seem very surprised, but he was most likely being polite. Then again, how did Ashtyn know his first and last name? I didn't remember ever mentioning it. Well, probably because of Uncle Rochon's last name, but that didn't explain how he said it.

Ashtyn walked away and paced a couple of times. "Mom! You don't know who this is?" He half-yelled, as if it was supposed to be obvious. We met the man recently; this was only the second time that Ashtyn had been around him.

"Yeah, he's Rochon's nephew. I told you we were coming here," I stated, unsure why he was so surprised.

Ashtyn's eyes finally left Airen and snapped my way. He dropped his arms, and the boy pointed at me. "No, you said we had to go with you on a playdate for Aubrey. You didn't say it was with one of the best linebackers God ever created, Airen Landry. You didn't, Mom. I promise, you didn't."

I looked up at Airen, trying to ignore his fine ass looking

how he was looking. "I'm so sorry. I still don't know what's happening." I laughed because I was so damn embarrassed at Ashtyn's ridiculous behavior.

Airen leaned in the doorway, watching with a minor grin before finally letting me in on the secret behind my son's reaction. "Looks like you have a football fan on your hands." Airen cheesed at my son acting a fool at his front door.

My head jerked back as my eyes connected with Airen's. "What does that mean? You play football?" I asked.

"No, he retired like three years ago. Dad was soooo mad. He loves you. You are seriously his favorite player. We both have your jersey."

"Really, Airen?" I lightly bumped his arm. "I bet you weren't gonna tell me either."

Airen shrugged and smirked in the sexiest way. "Eventually."

"Ma! He's going to be in the Hall of Fame one day. No question. He's won four Super Bowls with two teams. Are you serious? Is this really you? This is really your house? We're hanging at Airen Landry's house today?" All of it ran together as he looked everywhere but at us.

"Boy, slow down. Can we get inside the house before we melt?"

Airen laughed and opened the door all the way so we could step inside. For a football player, his home did not showcase his career. It made me think of reasons why. I'd be proud of my success if I were in his shoes. Looked like a little someone gave him more pride than the game. Displaying her was obviously more important.

Ariyah was on many of the walls — from baby pics to each milestone and birthday. That stood out to me the first time we were here. Nothing screamed football. As soon as we entered, baby girl came rushing down the stairs.

"Slow down, Ri," Airen cautioned. She obliged. "We don't need your playdate to start in the emergency room."

Once Ariyah made it to my little crew, she opened her arms wide and crashed into me. "Hi, Miss Khaliyah! I prayed we would see you again, and now you're here."

"Aww, hey to you too, cutie pie." I knelt to match her embrace.

Ariyah's hug felt like an angel wrapped its arms around me. Believe it or not, it felt like love. I kissed her cheek when we released each other.

"Aubrey! I missed you." She loved on my baby girl as much as she loved on me. "You wanna play in my room?"

"Yes!" Aubrey agreed. She gave me a look asking for permission.

"Go ahead." I kissed my munchkin. "Have fun."

Ashtyn finally snapped out of his trance as he explored the massive foyer with his brother. "Do you have a trophy room? Can I see your Super Bowl rings? Are you—"

"Boy, slow down." I gently popped his bird chest.

Airen laughed. "It's cool. I can give y'all a tour if you'd like." His eyes stayed on me a little too long. "We didn't get a chance to finish the tour last time."

I broke away first, giving my attention to my boys, and nodded. "Sounds good."

Airen led the way to the first space behind the stairs. It opened up to a high-ceiling living room. Then, the sliding wall to the backyard featured a pool that drove the boys crazy. They talked about jumping off the waterfall if they ever swam here. Trees lined the property line and gave Airen a ton of privacy.

Back inside, we ventured through the kitchen and saw Airen's office. That sucker had a lounge area, a wet bar, and a mini fridge. That's where Ashtyn got to see some football memorabilia. So far, that was the only room that displayed anything related to football—a room I missed during my first tour.

Upstairs, we visited the girls playing in the room of most little girls' dreams. It was truly fit for the little princess on Airen's hands. He pointed to his room on the other side of the house and mentioned the other four bedrooms we hadn't seen. The theater was top-notch and decorated perfectly. It was my favorite room.

Airen saved the best for last. Well, at least for the boys. We toured the game room made for them, even though it wasn't. "Whoa!" came from both of them when we turned the corner down the hall from the girls. Gaming systems, pool table, air hockey, basketball arcade game, recliners...you name it. This was a room made for someone who never wanted to leave home. There was also a balcony that looked over the backyard.

"Y'all gotta keep this all a secret. I'm tryna stay on the low right now," Airen told my sons.

"Yes, sir." Ashtyn walked around the room, touching everything gently. "My dad would trip if he knew you liked my mom. He's such a jerk to her."

"Ashtyn!" I yelled.

Ashtyn's hands rose with his shoulders. "What? Mom, you know it's true."

"Maybe, but you don't have to tell my business. Plus, this is a date for the girls to play. Airen doesn't like me like that."

"Says who?" Airen asked, winking at me.

The boys snickered. "Oh, don't get them started. Y'all go play." I waved toward the teen's dream room.

"There's juice and water in the mini-fridge and snacks in the cabinet next to it," Airen informed them.

"Cool," Aydyn said before turning on the TV. "Mom?" He failed to whisper as he pulled me to the side. "Can we come here for Halloween? I bet they give king size candy in this neighborhood."

"Boy! No," came out without giving his question any thought.

Airen cleared his throat and eased himself closer to us. "I'm not tryna eavesdrop. You gotta work on your whisper skills." Airen smiled at my son. "I'm cool with you guys coming here if your mom is. Maya usually takes Ariyah trick-or-treating. She brings in more candy than she can eat."

I narrowed my eyes at the man. "Why would you tell him that?"

"What?" Airen shrugged. "It's the truth. Let them have fun and stock up on free candy. We can even hang afterwards. Play games or whatever. I really don't mind."

"Of course, you don't." I bumped him with my hip

Ashtyn jumped in the conversation. "So, is that a yes? Please?" He stood next to his brother as they both pulled the pitiful look they wore to get their way. It rarely worked on me but this time I made an exception.

"Fine," I answered.

"Yes," the boys high-fived each other before thanking the man in the room. They left us to explore the games near the entertainment center.

Airen leaned toward me. "Do you mind going downstairs with me, or do you want to stay up here with the kids?"

"We can go downstairs. It doesn't seem like we're needed, anyway." I looked at the boys. "Please don't tear this man's stuff up."

"We won't." I heard their answers but missed their eyes. They were too distracted.

Airen placed his hand on my back as we turned to leave the boys. "You may not be able to get rid of us now."

He side-eyed me before leaning in closer. "Sounds like a plan." He smiled, asking for trouble.

This man was going to be a handful.

SEVENTEEN

Airen

I POURED a glass of whiskey for each of us. It was all I had right now. I'd forgotten to get wine for her. I handed her the glass and watched her sniff it. "You think I'm tryna drug you?"

She giggled. "No, I'm checking how strong it is."

"With your nose?"

"Yes. You have a problem with that?" She dared me with her big brown eyes.

"Not at all."

"Good, because I didn't care either way."

"Well, damn." I laughed.

Khaliyah took the tiniest sip and moved her tongue around her mouth. Then she nodded in approval before taking a full sip.

"You are a trip."

"Sometimes."

We sat in silence for a few seconds. I had to understand something, but wasn't sure how she'd answer. Either way, I was about to find out. I cleared my throat and sat in view of her facial features to see how she'd initially react. "So, your ex is a jerk?"

Khaliyah looked like she wanted to laugh, but didn't. "Um, kinda."

"I mean...for your son to say so. It must be a definitive yes."

Her nose wrinkled. I wasn't sure if it was from my response or the topic. I wanted to find out more about her.

"Ashtyn and Aydyn have seen the good and the bad. Their opinions are pretty accurate. Christian is an asshole, but he puts on somewhat of a front around the kids. They haven't seen how much of a so-called jerk he's been lately."

"Do you mind if I ask why you're not together?"

"I don't mind." She tapped her nails against the glass in her hands. "We might spend a lot of time together, anyway. Because of the girls, of course." She smiled, then raised the glass to her lips and drank. "In a nutshell, I wasn't cut out to be the wife he wanted. Life happened, and my perspective changed when I had my babies. He didn't like the changes."

"Like?" I asked, needing more information. I hoped she'd be willing to expose what most people didn't when a relationship falls apart. I was one of most people.

"Like...I graduated with a software engineering degree. By then, we already had Ashtyn, and Aydyn was on the way. I finished school because I refused to drop out. When I failed to lock down a job while pregnant, I waited until I had Aydyn. Then things were good. I started working in my field, and the boys thrived in daycare and school. Then, there was a bullying issue with the boys' school, which made me go the home-school route. I quit my job and did what I thought was best.

"It was a selfish decision, but I tried to make up for it. My ex's main thing was not having a stay-at-home wife who reaped the benefits of his labor. He said stay-at-home moms were lazy women who were basically another kid playing house while the husband dealt with adult life."

Not believing what she'd just explained, I said all I could, "That's a fucked up way of looking at it."

"True. I figured my time at home made him resent me, but I sucked it up. I wanted to be with my boys, and we could afford it. In his mind, we were supposed to be this power couple. I was supposed to climb the ranks as an engineer while he worked at his parents' practice. Eventually, he'd open his own, and I'd have some brag-worthy position. I fucked it all up when I worked from home while homeschooling. That was the nail in the coffin."

"Wait, so that's how you ended up divorced? Nobody cheated, no abuse, or drug addiction broke y'all apart?"

"There was abuse. Verbal and emotional. He stayed because of the boys. I figured one day it wouldn't be enough with how he talked to me. So, I started my business and some side hustles that he laughed at. Now, those same hustles are how I provide for my family. He'll still never respect it or me. Right after Aubrey was born, which was a fluke from one drunken night reminiscing, we became emotionally detached."

My brain rattled with that one. From appearance and vibe alone, Khaliyah was definitely a catch. To think some nigga let her go because she wanted to be a good mom. I'd now heard it all.

The drama in my world before now was a lot, and how things fell apart with my marriage had merit. I guess everybody was different, but if I'd met Khaliyah first, she'd be everything I ever wanted. A good head on her shoulders, willing to sacrifice for her children, and a go-getter because that entrepreneur life ain't no joke.

"I'm sorry you experienced all of that." I truly was.

"Me too. Many people have gone through so much worse. I got my feelings hurt." She snickered. "I got off easy. My grandparents taught me my worth, so his words didn't break me completely. There are moments when I wonder if what he thought of me was accurate. His mindset and ways surprised me. However, I'm really living the dream now. I can take care of myself and my kids. That's all that matters."

"Sooo, a man in your life doesn't matter?"

"Oooh, you're either being nosy or you're scared to ask me what you want." Khaliyah laughed and finished her drink. "A good man God sends to me would be great, but I have three kids. Even if the guy does somehow find me, I'm sure he expects me to be solo. Once he sees the whole package, he'll bounce. Three kids are a lot to take on. I don't expect anyone to do it. So, I am fine being alone until after they are grown. Maybe I'll find some divorcee around my age or older because men my age probably won't go for me either."

"Damn, how old are you? Yes, I know it's not polite, but you're acting like it holds that much weight."

"I'm thirty-five. I've learned enough about men who like what they see but are turned off by the 'I have three kids' line. That's the first thing I say when a guy seems interested. It has deterred them so far."

"You didn't say it to me." Learning more about her personality, I only wanted to know her response.

"Because I say it to guys who are interested in me. You missed that part?"

"I heard you clearly."

"Yeah, okay." She tried to mask her blush, but I caught it. Our melanin could only hide the color, not the act. This woman had me ready to go against what I had planned and risk my heart again.

Her phone dinged, and as she explored the notification, I admired the gorgeous being seated across from me. The sexiest part of her besides her face were those damn thighs. She wasn't a skinny girl, which had my attention the first moment I laid eyes on her. Her waist matched the rest of her soft, plump body. I wanted to devour every inch.

Khaliyah didn't wear makeup. At least I hadn't seen her

with any on yet. Dark freckles sprinkled her deep brown skin. From what I noticed, they were only on her cheeks.

I must've zoned out, since I didn't realize she was now looking at me. "Why are you staring at me like that? I got something on my face?"

"No." Before saying what was on my mind, I wondered if it would turn her off and shut down these dates for our girls. Then again, she made me not care anymore. She was worth it—her rejection or acceptance. "You're stunning. Your freckles are intoxicating."

"I don't have freckles." She covered her face. "They're moles. They keep popping up the older I get."

"Really? They look like freckles."

She dropped her hands on her lap. "Nope, if you get close enough, you'll see. It started off as only three and then, over the years, they multiplied and spread."

"They're beautiful. A unique feature on an already gorgeous woman."

Her shoulders relaxed as her head tilted to the side. I wanted so badly to feel her pursed lips on mine. A part of me was confident that I would.

Khaliyah kissed her teeth. "Man, who are you tryna fool? I know my aunt told you I don't play games."

I chuckled at the accuracy. Those were Maya's exact words. "The only game I play or played was on the field. I'm only stating facts." I raised my hands in surrender.

With a smile on her face, she bit the inside of lip. "Okay, fine. Thank you for the compliment, sir."

"Why do you call me sir? You think I'm a lot older than you?"

"No." Khaliyah's shoulders hunched, then dropped. "It's something I say. I'll stop if it bothers you."

A few shakes of the head as I swallowed my drink, I reassured her, "It doesn't."

She narrowed her eyes and kept them on me. "Hmm."

I tried not to read too much into it and ceased the questioning. Changing the subject to my current interest, I asked, "What kind of food do your sons like? I can order in. Pizza may be too played out."

"Ha!" Her loud ass laugh snatched my attention. "I know you don't have boys, but you were once a teen. Pizza is a major food group for them. I'm the one who forces them to eat other things. Otherwise, they'd eat pizza three times a day. But..." She nodded slowly. "I will allow it today."

"You sure? We can get something else. I'm not tryna mess up your routine."

"Pizza is perfect for the kids. I'll pick myself something on the way home."

My head jerked back. "Why not eat here?"

"Because I want to get comfortable and eat."

Still confused, I asked her, "Whatchu tryna do? Eat naked?"

"No! Oh, my goodness. I meant I take off my shoes, maybe even some undergarments, then I get comfy with a glass of something mildly strong with a good movie on. Well, at least when we have our free night. That's when we all do our own thing separately."

"Do your thing. I'm not gonna stop you."

"Um, I'd rather not. Pizza will suffice. I will get my time at home. Here, I have to keep my eye on you and the kids. Guard up." She raised her fist.

"I hear you. We aren't that close yet. One day, I wanna take part and remove some undergarments while watching a movie." I winked.

I couldn't help but laugh when her hand flew to her chest.

"Mr. Landry, you are something else."

"Sometimes." I used her line.

I ordered four pizzas. Two were with split toppings.

Everyone liked something different. I wasn't used to so many preferences and personalities. Her kids were well-mannered but silly as hell.

Ashtyn and Aydyn went at each other a lot. Each one trying to outdo the other with embarrassing antics. I learned a lot about their father; they kept comparing us. Ashtyn was the oldest, and he showed it. I could already tell that he was his mother's protector.

The night had come before I could get more alone time with Khaliyah. Something about her had me on edge. I wanted to see her again, but couldn't tell if she felt the same. Instead, I'd wait it out and feel my way around. Playdates would have to do for now.

I tried to talk myself out of the possibility of us, but it didn't work. Times like these, when I witnessed her in her element as a mom, I'd want nothing more than to have her in our lives. My guard dissipated in her presence, yet I felt the need to tread lightly in order to protect her.

Khaliyah's doubts about love and relationships were valid simply because of her boys. The man she created them with didn't have favor in their conversations. A distinct way to lose the "hero" view from your kids was to constantly fuck up in front of them or with them. According to Ashtyn and Aydyn, the way they witnessed their father threaten their mother was enough.

As the stranger coming in, I had to play it safe until I was sure her kids were even cool with the idea. I'd never want them to see me in a negative light when it came to their mother. Khaliyah had to be open to the idea of trying again, and her sons needed to trust me with her heart just as much as I needed her to.

EIGHTEEN

Airen

I HAD some free time on my hands and decided to put it to good use. I called up my uncle to have the conversation I'd avoided since he tried to introduce me to Khaliyah. Aunt Maya babysat Ariyah on her day off.

Both of them were successful business owners, yet they still made time for me and my daughter. I appreciated them for life. I'd always honor both of them like they were my parents.

Aunt Maya was a commercial real estate agent. Her brokerage was small, but she had the right people who brought in big money. The connections she'd gained over the years were a blessing to anyone she loved, including me.

One thing I'd learned in life was that God worked through people more than I ever realized. Growing up with Victor helped set me up financially. My original passion brought his firm clients back in the day.

Maya built a business that would ultimately find me a site for my rec center. August made connections that were linked to me. Now she's well-respected in the sports entertainment industry. I could go on forever.

All things worked together for our good. Neither of us started life knowing we'd be where we were today.

If I wasn't sure about anything else, I'd die declaring that God knows what He's doing. Sometimes I have to remind myself when it gets hard, but it has yet to be proven otherwise. Being still can be difficult, but every good thing from God was worth the refining process to get there.

Maya married a man who owned a construction and renovations company. If anyone ever asked me, the two of them were meant to be. Catching them at the same time to discuss plans was another story. She refused to talk business with me unless in a business setting. She was strict about keeping things separate with family. We had to schedule appointments during business hours.

When I reached my uncle, he agreed to meet me at Oliver's Grill for a quick lunch. Victor allowed me to dine where his family dined. A back room with a separate entrance. Luckily, his wife enjoyed her privacy just as much as I did. Because of my friendship with Victor, the perks extended to me.

Uncle Rochon came through the back of the restaurant and joined me at a table in the private room. There were four booths and two tables for four in here.

"What's up, youngin'? Why are you avoiding Maya?" was the first thing he asked as he scooted his chair up to the table.

I laughed, feeling like he'd read right through me. "Unc, I'm not avoiding her. There's something I wanted to talk to you about. Without her input," I rushed that last part.

Uncle Rochon cracked up. "Look, I know my wife. I understand." He rested his elbows on the table, covering his mouth with his fists. "So, this must be personal."

Nodding, I confirmed, "It is."

"Okay, then. Let me have it. What's going on?" The concern on his face made me rethink the secrecy. I wasn't trying to scare him.

"I think I'm ready for the talk."

His head quickly shook in shock and confusion. Unc

laughed. "Boy, I think it's too late for that. You have a whole daughter. The hell?"

I dropped my head and chuckled at his interpretation. If I recall it right, he was the one who had "the talk" with me when I was a teen. Two, to be exact. The birds and the bees and being a Black man in America.

"No, Unc." I leaned back in my chair, contemplating how to admit he was right without actually saying it. Before I opened my mouth, Victor texted me to send my order so he could get it to the right person. Only a few employees knew of my presence here. After asking my uncle what we wanted, I sent the message.

"Now, you gonna tell me what I'm here for or what?" he asked, slowly losing patience.

"Remember when you said you'd have to talk to me if I was interested in Maya's niece?" I reminded him. He dipped his chin and smirked. "Well, this is me officially interested. Should I even try?"

Unc smiled like I had just turned my life over to the Lord. He grabbed his phone and typed something quickly before setting it face down on the table. "First and foremost..." He held his hand out. I shook it reluctantly. "You won me a straight week of pampering from my wife."

"What?"

"Yeah, we thought the both of you were too damn stubborn to see what we see. Maya swore that she'd help Khaliyah open her eyes. I bet you would fold first."

"You bet against me? Damn, Unc."

"Not exactly. This bet attests to you being less stubborn than Khaliyah."

I shrugged. "I guess so."

"To answer your question, yes. Shoot your shot, as you youngin's say. She's a keeper. So, only go after her if you want the real thing and want it forever."

"Forever, huh?"

"Yep. She's the marrying type. Even though she's in that same lie, claiming that she doesn't want love." He dipped his chin, adding, "You're both on that wagon."

I straightened up in my seat and admitted, "I'm contemplating jumping off. She is exceptional in every aspect I've witnessed so far. We've talked a bit about her ex. I don't want to mess up before I start. Can you tell me anything about her that could help? Maybe give me a bit of an advantage. Whatever it is, I won't do it only to get her attention. I will be consistent, I promise."

"Oh, I heard about the roses. Good touch." Unc tilted his invisible hat to me. "Unfortunately, Maya knows everything. I can say that the fool who divorced her didn't do too much damage. She stayed true to herself, according to Maya. You see, my wife came out of her first marriage very different from how she went in. Her experience convinced her that all men were the same, and I initially paid the price for that mentality."

"Oh, yeah?" This was the first I'd heard of any issues between my favorite couple.

"Absolutely!" Unc spread his arms across the table before releasing a concerned sigh. "My baby was worth it, so I stayed patient. I prayed for her and with her. She was the first in her family to get a divorce, and she tried to punish herself for it.

"Our family was familiar with people leaving relationships. Hers wasn't. Maya's sister was her first experience with a significant absence, but marriages didn't end in her family. So, in her mind, something was wrong with her for her husband to leave her with three kids. She had no job, no degree, no money, or assets. Her family had to live with her parents for a few years before she got on her feet.

"Then I came along. My ex and I had been divorced for at least four years. I had business in Houston and ran into this smart-mouth woman from a networking event at a bar. I watched for a while before stepping to her, and she shot me all the way down. Maya was a man-hater, but there was a light on her I could not shake. I needed her around me. Her fire enticed me to take on the challenge. She thought her kids would scare me off. Then she attempted the tough route, but I saw her.

"Eventually, I sat her down as my friend and told her what I wanted and why I thought she was the one I wanted it with. I shared my vision, the role I imagined her playing, and what I wanted to be for her and her children. They were almost grown by then. Man, that woman finally broke down and showed her vulnerable side; the rest was history. I stuck with it because God placed the desire for me to be her person and for her to be mine. I couldn't shake her."

"Wow. I didn't know that. How did you even become friends?"

"I hired her former firm and demanded that she be my contact point."

"That's why you left?"

"Yep. Maya had her kids, and I wanted to be there for her. When they left the nest, she followed me back home."

"But y'all came back here."

"Her parents are getting older. She wanted to be close. She's the only daughter who stayed."

"Damn."

"Look, it was tough the first few months, then she got it together. Khaliyah had her aunt and others to keep her grounded in reality instead of being strung along in a lie sold by her ex. Those are Maya's words. Did the man hurt her? Yeah, but he didn't break her. So, like I said, she's a keeper. If you're serious, be serious and face the music."

"Face the music?" I asked, but the answer was immediately revealed as it exited my mouth. "You mean I really gotta admit this to Maya?"

"Yep. She's thrilled about it. If you hadn't noticed, my phone's been blowing up. So when you pick Ariyah up, be ready."

"I hear you."

He snickered a bit, trying to cover his mouth. "Your big ass really called me to tell me you're digging Khaliyah? You don't need help in that department. Then again, I can understand you wanting to be perfect but there's no such thing. Be honest. Don't try to be anything more or less. If she likes you, let it be the real you."

Our food came, and we enjoyed a meal, discussing his struggles with Aunt Maya. She gave him the business, and no one would have ever known by looking at them. For the first time, I had hope for what they had.

Unc had a couple of errands to run before he headed home, so I'd have to face his wife alone. I'd bet money he didn't have to do a damn thing. He wanted me to do this on my own.

I parked near the curb since Ariyah was drawing all over the driveway in chalk. Ariyah did the same routine that warmed my heart like it was for the first time. "Daddy!" she yelled, running and jumping into my arms. Her umbrella hat poked me in the forehead when I lifted her up.

"I see Aunt Maya got you covered from the sun."

Ariyah nodded and smiled. She tapped her hat. "It keeps me safe and cool."

"Just not cool looking," I snuck in before tickling her.

"I'm always cool."

I kissed her cheek and put her down. "Yes, you are."

My eyes landed on Maya, who didn't hide the grin on her damn face. "Woman, why are you looking like that cat from that movie?" She knew which one.

Aunt Maya burst out laughing. "Boy, shut up. Sit down

and listen, so I can help win my niecy's heart. If you break it, I will break you. Understand?"

"Yes, ma'am."

NINETEEN

Khaliyah

AFTER STUFFING my face with my servings from the baked potato bar Gammy created for this Sunday's dinner, I plopped on her couch. One of the greatest perks of living near my family was the many meals I didn't have to cook for myself. I had a cooking family. Taking advantage of these not-great-for-my-waist dinners meant I'd spend more time in my garage gym, but it was completely worth it.

Gammy smacked my leg when she sat next to me. "Owww! What I do?" I rubbed my throbbing thigh.

"What I tell yo' ass about jumping on my furniture? You gone break it."

I burst out laughing. "That hurt Gammy: my leg and my feelings. Why you act like your couch will snap in two? I know I gained weight, but you ain't gotta do me like that." I poked my lips in the biggest pout I could make.

"Girl, you look good. I've been telling you to stop plopping down ever since you were a little girl. You keep on doing it! You're too old, and so is my couch."

My suspicious side eye got me popped again. "Gammy!" I yelled in pain. "In the same spot?"

"Don't be looking at me like you wanna get popped, then."

"You can warn me first," I whined.

"That was the warning," she answered with her chin up. "Bet you won't do it again."

I rubbed my leg and kept my damn mouth shut. Aunt Maya snickered at my pain without coming to my defense. I mouthed "Get yo momma."

The boys were watching TV with my grandpa in the den. Aubrey was napping since I had her running around all day after getting home late last night. Once again, we left Airen's after midnight, and the girls still acted like they were sad.

Saturdays were usually our family night. The four of us played games, watched a movie, and ate junk food. We spent the last month of Saturdays with our "extended family"—the Landrys—the father-daughter duo.

My family knew about it since we kept skipping time with them. Last weekend revealed how much I loved spending time with Airen. He was safe.

Aunt Maya sipped her lemonade and smacked her lips loud as hell. "I'd help you, but I see you don't trust me anymore. So, nope."

"What I do?" I asked, giving my aunt my full attention.

"My favorite niece continues to lie to my face, and I don't like it."

I cracked a smile, confused. "I don't remember telling a lie."

"That's the thing about lying. You gotta keep up with so many to cover the first."

"Auntie, say what it is, please."

"You hooking up with Airen is what it is, Miss Thang."

My posture completely straightened. "Who told you that lie?"

"Don't make *me* pop you." She side-eyed me from across the room.

"I'm serious. I'm not with that man."

"So, you calling my Ariyah a liar?"

I dropped my head, trying to hide any blushing my melanin could reveal. I understood the confusion. "We've only had playdates. That means kids included."

"Mmmhmm. It starts that way."

"For who? When? The playdates were completely innocent. The girls love spending time with each other, and I don't want to leave my kids with strangers. End of story." I laid down and rested my head on Gammy's lap. She stroked my head like she used to do when I was a kid.

"What's the 4-1-1 with you and my nephew? You've been spending a lot of time with him. Don't lie and say it's only for playdates." Aunt Maya would not drop it. Mostly because she always knew when I lied, but this wasn't a lie. We weren't dating. She'd have to ask the right question for me to admit anything.

Trying to play it off, I scrunched up my face. "Eww, you made it sound weird. Your nephew and niece cannot date."

"Girl, shut up. Y'all ain't related! You like him, and you can't hide that fact. Your poker face falters when you speak of him. He's the same way about you."

I rolled my eyes until that last part registered. "Wait, what?" I lifted my head. "He said something about me?"

"Nope, but your excitement gave me all the answers I need."

"Ugh, fine! I like him. It doesn't mean he will go for someone with three damn kids!"

Gammy pushed my head off of her. I lifted myself and sat upright. Gammy said, "I'ma pop you again. Now, you're making excuses."

"But, Gammy, I—"

"I don't want to hear it! You are worthy of love, and so are your babies. The right man will accept all of you and treat you the way your husband should have. Even better. If you keep living with that mindset, you will be alone forever. That is not what you want. No matter how much you try to fool yourself."

Aunt Maya slow clapped loudly. "Exactly. Airen is a good man. I would never have considered him a possibility if I thought otherwise. Do yourself a favor and see where it goes."

I nodded my head, considering every word. It was time to open myself up to something beautiful. The past was over. I still had so much life ahead of me.

I closed my eyes. *God, please make it plain if he's who you want for me. I don't want to choose anymore. I need you to.*

KARINA CAME over for a bit of girl time. The boys were in the game room upstairs, giving us the living room. Aubrey was exhausted after school. She bathed before dinner, ate her food, and went straight to sleep.

My bestie kept bumping heads with her supervisor and had to get it off her chest. She convinced herself to quit her job. I tried my best to give her other options. If anything, she could ask to be assigned to a high school. That way, she'd keep a decent schedule and have light work.

"You are not the first person to say that. Guess I'll start looking tomorrow."

I lifted my wine glass toward her and clanked hers. "Good. Change will do you good."

Before she could respond, my phone rang. Airen's name appeared on my watch, and I declined the call, but not before Karina saw it. I sent him a quick text that I'd call him back.

"So, hubby checking in on you?" Karina winked with her goofy ass smile.

I dropped my head back on the couch. "Really? Why do y'all keep tryna marry me off like I need a man to be happy?"

"Of course you don't, boo. You desired a family before, and that doesn't go away because the one you chose the first time didn't work out."

"I have kids now! I need to be careful about moving forward if I choose to actually do it. Who I choose matters the most with my kids, since that person will be with us daily. I want to move forward carefully. Christian doesn't have to consider that. If I dated Airen, he'd be the first person since Christian. How are y'all so sure about him?"

"Because you care so much. You put your babies and healing first. You wouldn't jump prematurely. You weigh the pros and cons. The way you light up when you talk about him, it's so obvious to us. You've spent so much time with him and are still hanging out. That type of friendship makes these decisions easier. Your kids like him, too. It's not you fulfilling lustful desires and jumping on the first thing that shows interest, like somebody." Karina exaggerated "somebody." "You are careful and considerate. His bitch ass wouldn't consider no muthafuckin' body but himself, regardless. Let's be real about it."

I grabbed a grape from the fruit, cheese, and crackers tray I'd made. There was no need to argue with her. Especially since she was right. Those words hurt more than they should have. I chose him. I had hopes for a future with him. I created kids with him. And now, I was a single mother. Reality hits differently depending on the day.

Some days, I'm like fuck him. He didn't deserve me. Other days, I wonder if I could have done anything different to make him want me and see me as good enough to keep forever. Then he'd piss me off and I go back to the former.

Part of me wanted the hurt to pass. I wanted to be unbothered completely. The father of my kids has a new woman. They've been together about as long as we've been divorced and the shit hurt when I first learned about it. I don't even want him. I've learned the true Christian over the years and realized how much I didn't like him as a person. Nothing would keep me in that marriage with how he treated me. It still doesn't hurt any less to fail at something important to me.

I failed.

Now it was time to start over and try again. I deserved to be happy. Being in a healthy relationship and having a sane father figure for my kids was back on the table. Tomorrow, I might feel differently.

Was Airen someone who could fulfill that? I wasn't sure. I could no longer live in fear.

Maybe God created someone for us. He'd prepared us to endure Christian during the marriage and divorce. The healing process was hard and not one hundred percent complete, if that was even possible.

Everyone who loved me saw this man as I did—potential for forever. Pain and lack could have persuaded my hopes—a place where no decision should be made. With the advice from onlookers, the possibility of success wasn't all in my head.

I guess I'd find out one way or another.

TWENTY

Airen

ARIYAH REACHED the door before I did. She learned never to open it alone, but that knowledge meant nothing once she saw Aubrey on the security camera by the front door.

"Aubrey," she gushed once the barrier between them swung open.

The girls hugged like they hadn't seen each other the last three weekends in a row. I kept my attention on the girls as long as possible. Khaliyah's presence screamed, "Look but don't touch." I obeyed, mostly.

Even in shorts and a loose tee, the woman was the most gorgeous in existence. Her hair was in twists, hanging a little past her shoulders. I recall her describing the tedious task of styling her hair after embracing her natural texture. It fit her perfectly.

"What's up, Khaliyah?"

"Nothing much." Khaliyah's tone sounded a little heavy. I narrowed my eyes briefly, but didn't push. I may be wrong, but her energy seemed different.

My opened arms as I stepped closer forced her brow to hike. "If the girls can hug every time, we can too."

"Seriously?"

I nodded. "I want a hug, and you seem to need one."

"Mommy is the best hugger!" Aubrey informed me with a smile.

"Well, she has to prove it to me."

"Really? We've hugged before, Airen." I shrugged. Khaliyah playfully sighed with her big, beautiful smile on display. She glanced at the girls and surrendered. "Fine. Come here with your big ol' self."

Khaliyah closed the gap between us, allowing me to wrap my arms around her. Damn if I didn't want to hold her forever. When she exhaled against my chest, I wished these kids weren't here.

One moment too long, Khaliyah looked up at me. I let my eyes come down to meet hers. She opened her bite-worthy brown lips to ask, "Sooo, are you gonna hold me hostage in your arms all day, or are we going to the park?"

We laughed as I reluctantly released her. "You're right, my bad."

I squatted down to the girls and asked, "Are the most adorable princesses ready to take this playdate on the road?"

"Yeah!" they yelled in my face. That was on me. Two excited five-year-olds have no choice but to be loud as hell.

"Let's go," Khaliyah sang.

I led the ladies to the garage and opened all of their doors. Helping the girls get into my truck was a must, but Khaliyah almost needed a boost, too—my little Shawty Doo Wop.

We rode, blasting Pastor Mike Jr. all the way to the park. He was one of many artists we had in common. Finding good music to play around young kids and still enjoy was hard. Pastor Mike Jr. had an anointing on him because he made this grown man cry on many occasions, speaking life with his lyrics. Of course, he had some bangers that made old folks think I was in my car blasting cussin' music, as Unc called it.

Once we reached the park, I found an isolated spot near

the track and playground. It must've been perfect timing since no one else was in this area of the park.

We climbed out of my truck, and I helped our daughters. Khaliyah grabbed her backpack and met us on my side. Not even two seconds later, the girls asked to go on the swings.

Khaliyah answered for both of us before they took off to the nearby playground. The park had about four of them throughout.

"This is nice," Khaliyah told me as we strolled on the path of the track. "We have this entire area to ourselves. If I'm honest, I hate taking the kids to the park because I can't stand other people's kids."

I failed to hold in my laugh. "Damn, meanie. What about my daughter?"

She giggled. "Ariyah is a sweetheart. Most of the kids we encounter are smart assess who don't listen, and I don't want them anywhere near mine."

"Nah, I get what you're saying. I haven't had the issue yet since we only play with kids of friends or family."

"That makes sense. Aubrey is still very trusting. I'm slowly bursting her bubble about the real world. They've learned their lesson playing with other kids. My boys can now discern which ones to steer clear of so far. I've had to say something most of the time. These chirren be out here with no supervision, and I don't play that."

"I bet you don't. Mama Bear to the bone."

"Damn right. Anybody can get it. Kids too. I might accidentally trip or bump them into something. I can imagine myself falling on one if they piss me off enough."

Khaliyah had me cracking up. She said all that with a straight face.

"Lemme make sure Ariyah stays on her best behavior around you."

Her mouth fell open. "Shut up. I wouldn't really do it. I

just be thinking about it. Plus, Ariyah is respectful. I'm talking about these tablet-raised kids whose parents do not watch them or teach them anything. Life is real and can get busy, but we gotta do better with our kids."

The girls ran from the swings and climbed the ladder to the slide. For a moment, I had to remember not to hover. My first thought was to run over and make sure Ariyah got up there okay. Khaliyah had no sign of worry on her face, so I tried not to.

We stood near the playground but still on the track, watching the girls run, squeal, and laugh. The joy it brought to Khaliyah whenever the girls loudly displayed their happiness made a nigga feel all soft inside. I failed to identify the emotion, but it felt good. I could watch her watch them all day.

The footsteps of a lone runner from a distance came closer until they halted. I noticed him when we pulled up, but he was on the other end of the trail. "Yo! You Airen Landry," the man said. "Oh shit! Where the hell you been?" He paused for an answer, yet immediately filled the silent void before I opened my mouth. "Man, the game ain't been the same without you on my draft teams. My wallet misses you." He laughed, causing me to relax a little.

"Been laying low. Chilling with the people who mean the most to me." I rested my arm around Khaliyah's waist. Testing the waters a bit. She didn't pull away.

"That's real talk, bruh. I remember what your old lady did, man. I prayed for you. You're a good dude. I'm sorry you experienced all the mess and pain, man. I'm glad to see it didn't break you, brother."

"I appreciate you for that."

"A'ight, dawg. I'ma finish my run and let you and wifey enjoy your time out here. It was good to see you." He dapped me up and left us.

Khaliyah bumped me with her hip. "That was pleasant. I forgot you be out here ducking and dodging people. If you want to leave, we can." She looked up at me before her watchful gaze returned to the girls at the playground.

I shook my head. "We're good. This is a nice change. Being cooped up ain't my favorite, but it's been the safest."

"Hmm," was her only response. She leaned her head on my chest as we stood closer.

Something felt off in that moment. Even her breathing changed, not as relaxed. "What's on your mind?"

Khaliyah opened her mouth to speak, then closed it. The second time she did it, I needed to understand what she was afraid to say.

"I won't get offended if that's what's stopping you. What's up?" I glanced down at her, but could not see her face from this angle. I leaned back and faced her.

Her worried expression made me want to protect her from her own thoughts. "Khaliyah, say it. You're killing me, woman."

She shook her head. "I-I might be overthinking things."

"Under-think them then."

"What?" she laughed.

"I mean, simplify it. Did I upset you?"

"No! Nothing like that. You kinda changed my perspective on things. I'm not sure what it means."

Immediately, I somehow sensed we shared the same perspective. She evoked the same thing in me. "I might know." I searched her eyes, still filled with worry. "How about we start off as friends and see if we can uncomplicate things for each other?"

Khaliyah's sigh reassured me I was on the right track. Our pasts were obstacles that challenged what we felt versus what we'd learned from experience. She turned toward the girls again. "So, how do we become friends first? I'm not sure how to even do this anymore. Is it with the intention of something more or simply friends?"

Overthinking was definitely her go-to response. To ease her confusion, I answered, "Kind of how we're doing it now. Spend time learning about each other. We're basically attached at the hip now that the girls can't get enough of each other." We laughed. "Simply friends with companionship as the only benefit and expectation. Unfortunately, the exterior tends to determine compatibility for so many people. I don't want to love like that. It's gotten me nowhere."

"Don't I know it?" She rolled her eyes. "My children's dad's outer shell got my attention in college, but all the ugliness his shallow heart pumped out revealed his true character, eventually. I learned too late." She seemed lost in thought again before she raised a finger. "This means we aren't dating, right? We can date anyone while developing a healthy, meaningful friendship." I wasn't sure if she was still asking me or if she answered herself.

"What are you doing for Thanksgiving?" She asked.

I assumed she wanted to change the subject. I couldn't blame her. Especially if she was just as terrified as I was of where our friendship could lead. I answered, "Spending the day with Unc and Maya at your grandparents' house. I've had the pleasure of that normalcy the last couple of years. Me and Ariyah eat then leave early to decorate for Christmas in the evening. I don't see that changing this year."

She laughed. "I guess we'll be spending the holidays together."

"Yeah, you're not getting rid of us anytime soon."

"Wouldn't dream of it. We won't be ducking off early, though. Our family starts decorating the Saturday after."

As soon as the thought entered my mind, if came out of my mouth. "Maybe you can leave early this year. Come over and decorate with us. We'll return the favor."

Khaliyah raised her head to look me in the eye. "You sure? Traditions are serious business. Ariyah might wanna keep that between the two of you."

"Why do you think I'm asking? Ari wants to include you and your family in everything. Any time I bring up our plans, you are the first person she asks about. This is no different."

"I'll talk with the kiddos and see what they want to do. Knowing them, consider us there."

Aubrey and Ariyah ran toward us to get the bag Khaliyah held. She was much more prepared than I was. The girls grabbed two bottles of bubbles. "Mommy, can we draw on the ground?" Aubrey asked.

Khaliyah scanned the area. "Ooh, yep. We can go to that gazebo over there. Plus, I know you might want a snack too."

"Yay!" the girls yelled.

We made eye contact, and I followed her lead. When we settled at a table, Khaliyah pulled out hand sanitizer, juices, and a variety of snacks. She even had food for us. I grabbed a bag of popcorn.

Khaliyah held my hand and squeezed the sanitizer in my palm. That insignificant gesture had me ready to skip the friend phase. The woman was caring, considerate, and everything I asked God for if I ever ventured into the love pool again. I asked for things in a woman that would purposefully make her impossible to find. A series of playdates almost had my ass wide open.

To be sure about what I thought I already knew, we'd move slowly enough for Khaliyah to see all of me. It may not be as pleasant for her as I would think. Arrogance could play no role in our friendship, which meant it definitely had no place in our relationship. We had to become friends first before anything else. I wouldn't shortchange either of us of the real thing. As convinced as I was, we had to do this right.

That way, we will have the ending we wanted the first time around.

Halfway through my popcorn, I circled back to her question about us dating other people. She told me before that she wasn't really open to dating. I figured she didn't want me to wait on her if I thought the right woman came along during our friendship. If this woman only knew how impossible that scenario was. I allowed her to think I'd be open to others, so I wouldn't seem crazy admitting something we'd both be afraid of.

She was becoming my person.

A scripture suddenly came to mind that Uncle Rochon constantly told me when my life went to shit with Mercy and former players. It made sense. While Khaliyah got the girls situated with the chalk and other outdoor toys, I pulled out my phone and searched for the Bible app. I found James 1:2 and could hear Unc's voice when I read it. Then I switched to the NLT version, which is my preferred one.

...when troubles of any kind come your way, consider it an opportunity for great joy. For you know that when your faith is tested, your endurance has a chance to grow. So let it grow, for when your endurance is fully developed, you will be perfect and complete, needing nothing.

I'd learned to be patient with all the blows during and after my marriage. For a long time, I hated it when people would say my pain had a purpose. Especially when the pain came from a woman I did everything right by. I followed the rules, did my part, and more, but suffering always found me.

After Mercy, love seemed unattainable unless it came from certain family members. I wasn't dumb enough to think they all loved me. Unfortunately, that lesson hit worse than all of them. It was all part of life and strengthened my faith because I was still here.

"Whatchu reading?" Khaliyah pulled me out of my daze. I

showed her my screen. "The Bible?" She smiled. "What made you need a word right now?"

I didn't hesitate to answer with, "You. This moment. Our daughters. Thinking a little about how far Ari and I have come. Now we can enjoy such a ... a sweet and peaceful moment."

The smile on her face widened while her eyes held their connection to mine. I was open and vulnerable, and for two seconds, I would've given her anything she asked me for. What was up with this woman's hold on me? A single glance, and I was finished. Done.

Don't do anything stupid.

Take it slow.

Khaliyah pulled away first and rejoined the girls. Without looking at me, she said, "Peaceful is all I need."

TWENTY-ONE

Khaliyah

THE BOYS' birthdays were a year and three days apart. At some point, I thought they'd want to have separate parties. I was more than prepared to grant their request, but last month, they asked, "Can we have a gaming party at Mr. Airen's house?"

My first response was "Hell no!"

They came back at me with, "But Mr. Airen said it was okay if you said it was. Please?"

That warranted a call to the sexy giant.

"*Hey, you,*" he answered.

"*Sir, when were you going to inform me about throwing your home in the hat for my son's birthday party venue?*"

"*I'm having a magnificent day. How nice of you to ask. How's yours?*"

"*Airen Rochon Landry, I am not playing with you.*" His cackling on the other end of the phone made me smile, but he wouldn't learn of my amusement. "*Airen, for real.*"

"*I'm sorry. Nobody has called me by my full name since I was a child. How dare you?*"

"*Boy! How dare you? I'm not about to let these boys invade your privacy just because you choose to spoil them. Tell them no.*"

"Nope. Not gonna be able to do that. They asked. I answered honestly. I see no issue if they want to use my home for a family-only party."

"Maybe talking to me first would've caused no issue."

"Khaliyah, you can have the party here."

"Who said I was even going to invite you?"

"See now you tryna throw darts 'cause your feelings hurt."

"No, they are not." I lied. I was the party planner, the best gift giver, the thoughtful one. I'd had to deal with being outdone ever since I met this man.

Airen chuckled. "I've learned to know the difference. Your sons came to me first. You're not used to that. It's okay, pumpkin. They like me more."

"I—" I stumbled when the last part registered. "How am I supposed to compete with a freaking football superstar?"

"You can't." I imagined his broad shoulders lifted briefly.

We both laughed at his ridiculousness. "Airen, I cannot ask to use your home. You are more than welcome to come to my house for the party. I will make sure there's something for everybody to do. If we have outsiders, they will respect your privacy."

"Fine, woman. But if I may, would you allow me to plan it with you?"

"Plan what?"

"The party. I don't have boys. I want to be a part of putting it together."

"You're serious?"

"I am."

For a moment, I thought of all the reasons I should say no. Somehow, I answered, "Okay."

The party was in full swing on this Saturday afternoon. Ashtyn and Aydyn were now fourteen and thirteen, respectively. Family, including Airen and Ariyah, came over for cake and ice cream after school on each of their actual birthdays.

Airen turned my home into a retro arcade as a surprise for the boys. I had them spend Friday night with their great-grandparents while we set everything up here. Honestly, I barely had any say. My job was food and drinks. Karina had a friend with a intimate event decor business. We'd given Mariah, owner of Cherished Moments, a budget and theme. She did not disappoint.

My new best friend, as he called himself, installed two more large screens in my home to accommodate multiple gaming systems. He had four arcade machines, an anime Gashapon machine, and goodie bags I wanted for my damn self. That was the only way I could describe it.

Since the party was at my house, I allowed the boys to invite their classmates. Fifteen of the twenty invited guests showed up. Their reactions were as wild as my sons' an hour prior. Jaws on the floor, hands on top of their heads, and "whoa" being the only word in their vocabulary.

Parents were invited to stay but only a few did. One of the dads recognized Airen after having a conversation with him. He had the same respect and well wishes as the guy from the park. It only made me want to ask more questions about Ariyah's mom. He never seemed ready to talk about her.

I overheard a conversation with one of the kids asking Ashtyn why he never told him that Airen Landry was his dad. I noticed the brief sadness in his eyes when he admitted that Airen wasn't. We'd have to talk about that later. As much as I disliked their father, I never wanted them to wish another man was their father. Life happens and our experiences are all for some purpose that will make sense. Something I often had to remind myself of.

After playing a few card games with the women, we made plans to take all of our boys out somewhere after the holidays. They were good kids and we wanted to get more comfortable with each other. That way the boys could spend more time together outside of school. Befriending my sons' friends parents would ease my nerves when they'd ask to go to their house. It'd take a lot for me to let go, but I was hopeful.

I snuck up on my incog-negro buddy as he grabbed a water bottle from the fridge. "You've outdone yourself. Well done, sir."

He looked down toward me. "They deserve it."

"Yeah, well, you have officially won parent of the year and they're not even your kids."

"There are ways around that." Before I could respond, he asked, "Is Christian still coming?"

Way to ruin a good mood. I shrugged. "He's an hour late, so probably not."

"That's too bad. You have amazing kids, Khaliyah. I hope you know that you have done well by them."

I allowed my head to drop, bringing my attention to my nails. I nodded to acknowledge his statement, one I'd heard over and over from everyone but the person I created my babies with.

Airen's finger hooked my chin, forcing me to look at him. Before he spoke, he grabbed a napkin and dabbed the corners of my eyes. He cupped my face. "I didn't mean to upset you."

"You didn't." I rested my hand on the outside of one of his.

"Pizza's here," Karina yelled from the foyer.

I broke away from Airen to set up the food. These kids had been snacking on fruit, chips, popcorn, and cookies, so I knew they were ready for something more filling. I prepared wings and a salad bar for the adults if they didn't want pizza.

After the food, we sang Stevie Wonder's rendition of "Happy Birthday" before the boys waved the flames out on each of their cakes. Mariah's sister owned a custom dessert business called Treats by Leah B. By the "oohs" and "ahhs" from the appearance and the "mmms" after tasting them, we had two go to Black-Owned businesses for events from now on.

The three-hour party had finally ended. Only my family remained in the house. Airen planned to take the games and TVs back to his house tomorrow afternoon.

"Now *that* was a party," PopPop said.

"Who you telling? We had to force you to give the kids a turn at Pac-Man," Aunt Maya reminded him.

"Can a old man live a little? It's been decades since I'd seen that machine."

"Decades! You're old, PopPop," Ashtyn said, patting his great-grandfather on the back.

"Getcho child, Khaliyah." PopPop pretended to swing at my son.

Uncle Rochon and Aunt Maya kept their eyes on me and Airen. "You two make quite the team," Auntie stated with conviction.

Karina nodded. "I must agree. This was fun. I had to school some of these little fools at Donkey Kong."

"I'm glad you all enjoyed yourselves," I said. "The real question is, did Ashtyn and Aydyn have a good time?"

"It was the best!" Aydyn damn near yelled after coming up for air from one of the arcade games.

Ashtyn slowly made his way over to Airen. "Thank you, Mr. Airen." He offered his hand. Airen stuck his out too slow. "Sike!" Ashtyn yanked his hand out of reach.

Everyone chuckled at their play-boxing. Then Ashtyn stopped and stared at Airen. To all of our surprise, he wrapped his arms around Airen and held on tightly. We tried to ignore the fact that we heard Ashtyn sniffle when he turned his head away from us.

Aydyn caught on and joined the hug. "Thank you so much, Mr. Airen. This was the best birthday ever."

There wasn't a dry eye in the room. The girls were the only

ones absent. They'd fallen asleep in my bed watching a movie not too long ago.

Someone knocked on the front door. Karina yelled for them to enter, assuming Mariah had returned to pick up her things.

The sound of two sets of footsteps came through the foyer.

"Sorry, we missed the party," Christian said with gift bags hanging on one arm and his wife on the other.

The boys released Airen, but never moved away from him. I saw something for the first time in Airen's eyes — anger. Part of me understood why. We'd talked a lot about the man who showed up late, as if anyone would be happy to see him. Kaitlyn waved at everyone. No one moved a muscle or spoke a word.

I broke the silence. "Boys, go say hi to your father."

Ashtyn's expression sent chills down my spine. He was livid, but respectful enough not to act on it.

"Please," I mouthed.

My son's nostrils flared before he glanced at me and Airen. When he moved toward Christian, Aydyn followed his lead.

They side-hugged their father and spoke to his wife. Both immediately returned to Airen and me.

"Did I miss something? Why are y'all so quiet?" Christian asked.

PopPop snorted before answering. "If you hadn't noticed, the party is over. No one expected to see you at this late hour."

Christian sucked his teeth. "It's only eight, Allen."

"That's Mr. Hobbs to you," PopPop corrected him. "Eight is late for a party that started at four-thirty."

"Oh, damn. My bad...Mr. Hobbs. I guess Angelina is now Mrs. Hobbs, too?" He waited for an answer but got nothing. Aunt Maya folded her arms over her chest and posted up on the wall beside her husband. "Y'all still salty about me divorcing Khaliyah? That's old news. She must've lied to you about why if y'all treating me like this," Christian started with his bullshit.

"Like my daddy said, the party is over. If you'd like some cake, I'd be more than happy to pack you a piece and send you on your way," Aunt Maya told him.

Airen's eyes shifted between me, the boys, and the newly arrived couple. I couldn't imagine what went on in his head. Something about it made me feel safe with him near. Like I knew he'd protect me if needed.

As if he heard my thoughts, his eyes fell to mine. "You good?"

I nodded.

Christian looked at the boys. "I'm sorry we're so late. We were out celebrating our—"

"Boy, don't nobody care what you were celebrating during your sons' birthday party. We see where your priorities lie. Take the cake and go." Karina popped off.

"Who do you think—" Kaitlyn tried it.

"Oh, no you don't, Missy. We do not know you. Your husband should know better than to come here like this. The party is over," Gammy reiterated.

"Khaliyah, you ain't got nothing to say? Or does everyone else speak for you now? I'm here for my sons."

Airen grabbed my hand. My eyes welled up because everyone literally went into protective mode for me and my sons. I never asked them to or needed them to, but they loved us enough to know how much we hated interacting with this man.

"Thanks for the gifts, Dad," Aydyn spoke for himself and his big brother.

"You don't even know what's in the bag," Christian argued. "That's okay, son. I get it. Looks like you had one helluva party." He gestured at the decor and set up. "Glad my money is going to good use." Christian and his wife laughed alone.

Almost defeated, Aydyn leaned on Airen. His father's gaze landed on the hard-to-miss man attached to me by the hand.

"Is this the kissing cousin Aubrey told me about?" Christian had the assholedacity to ask.

"What?" came out of at least three of the adults' mouths.

Airen just studied Christian. I was grateful he didn't engage. I told him about Christian calling him a kissing cousin when Aubrey tried to explain who he was. We laughed it off then. Right now, Airen looked like he wanted to attack. Thank God for giving him the strength to hold it together.

Uncle Rochon questioned his wife under his breath, but loud enough for us to catch. "What did he say about my nephew?" Auntie waved off his inquiry. I assumed she didn't want this interaction to linger any longer with this fool in our space. The quicker he'd leave, the quicker we'd breathe and explain the ignorance, if possible.

"Do you need the boys to open the gifts for you? We're exhausted. Like you were told before, the party is over. They can open them so you can go." I stepped out in front of Airen, remembering the boys saying he was Christian's favorite player. Airen's hat did magic, but if he'd gotten any closer, I was sure he'd recognize him. There was no telling how he'd react.

Again, Airen must've read my mind. He removed his hat and rubbed his hand through his hair. Without a word spoken, he stood tall beside me.

My ex-husband's eyes bugged out like Ashtyn's when he met Airen. "Landry?" Christian looked at Rochon. "Your nephew is THE Airen Landry. And nobody ever told me?" He stepped to Airen and offered his hand. "It's damn good to meet you, man." Airen's brow hiked at the presumptuous gesture. He turned down the handshake, but Christian kept talking, disregarding the energy in the room. "I've watched your entire career. Even after your wife..." Christian snorted and rubbed his nose dramatically, then laughed. "Some people just can't handle the fame without that white, am I right?"

Airen turned toward me. His expression asked, "Was this guy serious?" I had no words. Airen remained stoic, even though his tight eyes and heavy breathing revealed his desire to hurt the man. I didn't blame him. "It'd be wise not to speak on things you know nothing about," Airen calmly said.

"I'm saying! The fuck is wrong with you?" Karina asked. "You're still an insensitive bastard. Sorry, boys." She remembered there were kids in the room. They shrugged it off.

Christian's smile vanished when no one else shared his excitement. His wife opened her mouth, but my aunt shot a look that shut her down.

"I think it's time for you to leave," Airen told him.

"Who are you to tell me to leave? My family lives here. Stick to football, my guy. We see how your family turned out." Airen's stance widened, his hands formed into fists, and his arms flexed. He'd had enough. The man hadn't said a word, which didn't seem like a good sign. His energy shifted, and it was my turn to protect him.

I grabbed Airen's arm and stood in front of him. "To spare my sons any more of your ignorance, get out. I'm not asking, I'm telling. Take your girl and get out of my house."

"Why you all bothered? You fucking the cousin?" Christian asked with a smug smile.

The commotion came from every other adult on my behalf. I turned to my boys. "Go to my room."

Ashtyn's chest heaved over and over. He threw his gift at his father's feet and left the room. Aydyn dropped his bag before following behind his brother.

Once they were behind the closed door, I stepped closer to my ex. Airen quickly wrapped his arm around my waist, halting my strides. "He's not worth whatever energy you're about to waste on him. Trust me," he whispered in my ear.

He was right. I bit my lip hard enough to let go of what I really wanted to do and say. "Goodbye, Christian."

"Always gotta make me the villain. I see you've been feeding them the victim bullshit as if you played no role in your failure. That's cool." He snorted. "I got the right one this time around." He pulled his Kaitlyn closer to him. "I don't need this shit."

Airen tapped my hip to remind me not to respond. Uncle Rochon walked up on Christian to follow them to the door and lock it afterward. When he returned, he looked at everyone and burst out laughing.

"Oh, I never wanted to fuck someone up so much in my life," he said, holding his chest.

"Who you telling?" Airen finally relaxed, but hadn't released me. "WWJD just saved my life and his." We cackled. WWJD has power over us even today.

"What an asshole?" Karina added. "Yet, he still thinks he's such a good person. He was about to get jumped."

We laughed again at the realness. All of us wanted to pop him at least one good time.

I rested my hand on Airen's arm, still around me. "You can let go of me now."

"What if I don't want to?" He rested his temple against mine.

I turned to get a good look at his face. "That's because the beauty blinds you." I chuckled. "Save yourself like he did. Find someone better. The right one. It's never gonna be me. For anybody."

Airen's eyes narrowed as if I'd called him out of his name.

I pulled away from him and resumed cleaning the kitchen. My family stayed for another hour before leaving us. Airen apologized to my sons for their father and took Ariyah home.

He said very little to me. I'd given him a spare key to my house so he could get his things while we were at church.

I embarrassed myself with my comment, especially after witnessing his reaction. It was a bad habit of mine that he didn't deserve to see.

TWENTY-TWO

Airen

AUGUST CAME over after I dropped Ariyah off at school. She sat in with me as the guys and I recorded another episode. Her little ass would have to be edited out more than before.

Izak called her out. "This show is about the three of us. When did you become the fourth host?"

"I'm sorry. I got excited. This is fun, but you're right. Bye." She excused herself from my makeshift recording room.

After another thirty minutes, we finished the episode. I found August snooping around in my office.

"You looking for something?" I asked abruptly.

She jumped and shrieked. "No. I'm bored, Airen." The woman pouted.

"What? I'm sure you had something to do or somewhere else to go."

"Not really. I took the day off. Boredom called me to your house after Matt went to work and the kids left for school. I already got everybody's Christmas gifts. You know I shop early. What do I do with all this free time?"

"Not punish me for it." I leaned against the wall by the door.

"Screw you. You love me." August walked over to the coffee table where she'd found my next drop-off gift for

Khaliyah. "Ooooh! Is this for the next Mrs. Landry?" She fawned over the gift basket I put together.

"It's none of your concern."

August gasped. "You didn't deny it! You're falling for her?" Her eyes widened when I gave no response. "Oh my gosh, oh my gosh, oh my gosh. Airen!" She bounced in her seat on my sofa.

"Chill out. I'm doing something nice for a friend."

"Oh negro, we have been friends for more than a decade and you ain't EVER sent me nothing like this."

"You're right. I only..." I played coy. "Referred half of your client list to you. My bad. I'll do better and get you a basket."

I got hit with a pillow for that one. "Shut up. You get what I mean."

"Do I?"

"You get on my nerves. Thank you for the referrals. I guess you have to give love the way it's needed. You did well, brother. Now, why does Khaliyah need all of this? Did you do something stupid?"

"No, she did."

August leaned back, getting too comfortable. "What she do?" she whispered with her nosy ass. She'd bug me until I spilled it.

I gave her the rundown of the previous weekend. Khaliyah hadn't said a word to me in days. I assumed she was mad at me, but I learned from Maya that she was angry with herself. The dumb ass comment she made pissed her off too. I kept quiet because I hadn't made my intentions known. Our new friendship meant I had to stay in my lane. For now.

"Is she not over her ex?" August asked a question I struggled with after I left Khaliyah's house that night. After my conversation with Maya, I had more clarity.

"I think she's in denial about wanting happiness in a relationship."

"Ha! Sounds like someone I know."

"Shut up."

"What? Don't be mad now that you have to deal with yourself. Well, the female version. It's frustrating, ain't it? That's exactly what you get."

"I do not like you. Get out of my house."

"Nope. Admit that you're falling for her, then I'll drop it."

Falling was a stretch. We were in the learning phase, and that was only because of our kids. We had no expectations. Friendship was all we had to offer so far. This was my first opportunity to show up as her friend outside of our kids. I wasn't falling. I was...leaning.

"Mind your business, and you get to keep me as a client."

"Negro, please. You ain't going nowhere." True. August dug into the basket. "Gift cards!? Damn, you put a grand on each. You tryna buy her?"

"Hell, no. I'm merely forcing her to get some things for herself."

"Women like her aren't good at receiving expensive gifts. It's clear since she won't even receive you being there for her. So, let me hold on to a few of these cards. You know my boys suck at gifts." I gave my answer by looking at her like she was crazy. "I want a basket customized with love, too. What if she doesn't even shop at these places?"

"She does. I got confirmation from her aunt and best friend."

"So, they are in on it, too. Yeah, you're falling. Ain't no way you doing this for nothing. I know how you fools think." She searched more into the basket that didn't belong to her. "You considered everything! Lotions, socks, face masks, and body scrubs. Damn, she got you sprung."

"If caring about a person's well-being makes me sprung, then boing, boing."

August fell back laughing. "You're so corny." She

rearranged the basket a bit. "So, when will I finally get to meet her?"

"At some point. Let me make sure we're good first."

"I'm sure y'all are. I can't wait." After putting everything in place and making the basket look better than before, August smiled at her work. She sighed when the gurgling of her stomach filled the silence. "You wanna get something to eat?"

"Sounds like you do."

She chuckled. "Forget you."

"I can eat. As long as you're buying."

"Yeah, right. You got it. Tell Victor we on the way. I know what I want to order."

WHEN AUGUST and I returned to my house, she left. I called Kaliyah to make sure she was home. I told her I had to give her the house key back and was on the way, then hung up. I didn't want her to say anything until we were face-to-face.

We hadn't made plans this weekend for the kids to hang out. I needed to ensure she wasn't still upset with herself or thought I was.

Did her comment piss me off? Initially, yes.

How could she tell me to save myself from her?

I wasn't mad anymore. I wanted an explanation and the opportunity to help remove that insecurity if she allowed me to.

After knocking, I waited a short time before she opened the door. She wore sweat shorts, a hoodie, and long fuzzy socks.

"Hey," she answered somberly.

"Hey, yourself."

Khaliyah's eyes grew twice in size. "Another gift basket?

Airen, you have to stop. You act like you did something wrong." She turned around and walked away. I followed her to the kitchen. "I'm the one who should be apologizing."

"You should. More to yourself than to me, though."

The way her ex waltzed in like the world waited for him to arrive was all I needed to see. Then he opened his mouth, and all I wanted to do was bust him in his shit. As good as it would've felt, the boys deserved an example of better behavior. Growing up with the type of father they had, I wouldn't dare fall to his level and disappoint them in that way.

After spending months with this family, I longed for their permanent presence. They brought peace to my life in a way that made no earthly sense. Supernaturally, God covered them with exactly what my heart desired and placed them in my path.

Uncle Rochon would swear up and down that circumstances always had a purpose. In the storm, all we could do was trust God. When the storm ended, the light revealed all the work God had his hand in, and the pain made sense. Khaliyah and her kids slowly helped me see the purpose of my pain. A complete family was possible.

Until I was ready to share my desires with Khaliyah, she'd still have me in the most important role I could have in her life right now—her friend. A redefined role for both of us. As much as I needed her, I also wanted to be there for her. I didn't have her whole story yet, but soon enough, I would. Her guardedness was justified, from what I had seen.

She looked at me with eyes full of regret. "I am."

I set the basket down on the countertop. "Let me hear you say it."

"Say what?"

"Why are you sorry?"

Khaliyah's shoulders dropped as her head fell to the side. "Airen, you don't have to do this."

"As your friend, I do. You don't truly believe what you said to me, right?"

"Why does it matter?"

"Because I care about you. No friend of mine will talk down about herself in front of me and get away with it."

"Ugh, fine. I'm sorry that I said what I said. I didn't mean it completely. I have my moments."

I'd annoyed her enough for the time being. I let go of the urge to unpack her statement. "I forgive you."

"Good. No more baskets. You spoil my kids enough. You don't need to spoil me. This is the third one!" She pulled out some of the gift cards. "Oh, hell no! This is too much, Airen."

"For who? I'm not taking it back. Accept the gift."

"I have to repay you."

"It's a gift. No, you don't."

"I do." She pulled out hand creams and socks. "I don't deserve this."

"Looks like you need more gift baskets. You ain't learned your lesson."

Khaliyah burst out laughing. She'd finally appeared happy, even for a moment. I'd take what I could get. It'd take more time to get her to stop being so damn negative.

I've had the displeasure of meeting her ex and understood immediately that she deserved to treat herself better. Until she learned how, I'd continue to remind her.

Ashtyn and Aydyn witnessing it all made things worse. It was my dream to have sons I could play ball and roughhouse with, to have younger versions of me look to me for advice, and model how a good man lives regarding himself and those around him. What they'd seen with Christian was nothing of the sort. I prayed that even if their mother didn't see me as I saw her, I could be in their lives. They'd need it.

I found the woman before me as stubborn as I'd been warned. After seeing things firsthand, I low-key understood why she'd push me away. When a terrible partner was all you'd ever known, trying again seemed daunting and not worth it. We were in the same boat on that front. Being the one who wanted in made me view relationships differently. She had me open to it.

"Are you going to keep avoiding me?" I asked. "Ri needs to know more than anyone." I smirked at her not buying it.

Khaliyah sat on a barstool. "Airen, that was so embarrassing. I'm not for the drama. It seems to follow me around whenever my kids' father is near. Then you thought you had to stand up for me, which made me feel awful. Like I was dragging you into the mess."

I leaned back on the counter opposite her. "You are going to be a handful, woman." She dropped her head. "Nope. Look at me." She raised her head, locking eyes with me. "Are we not friends?"

"We are, but—"

"Mm-mm. On the rare occasions when I make friends, they become family. People I can count on and who can depend on me. As your friend, I had every right to step in. No harm done."

"Yeah, but now he knows who you are."

"Is that supposed to scare me?"

"Airen, you are extremely private for valid reasons. He is a top tier petty ass person. I don't want your comfort snatched away because of his asshole tendencies."

"Khaliyah, the most the man can do is tell people I'm in Houston. So fucking what? It's worth protecting you."

She rolled her eyes in defeat. "You say that now."

"I mean it. If it ever comes down to it, I will face whatever. Ain't nobody knocking down my doors or following me around. We good."

"I'm sorry for everything." The woman still looked defeated like she'd somehow hurt me. "How about you and

Ari come over on Christmas Eve? I will even cook for you. Consider it my gratitude for you caring enough to do all of this. I want to do something for you even if you say I don't need to."

"You're not gonna let it go, are you?"

"I'm really not. So, you might as well say yes. We can share another one of our traditions with you guys."

"We'll be there."

Khaliyah smiled until she pulled more cards from the basket. "I cannot believe you spent all this damn money on me when I'm the one who messed up. Who does that?"

"A friend who wants you to feel better and not beat yourself up over nothing."

"That usually comes in an inspirational text or in-person conversation. Not thousands of dollars' worth of gifts. Don't make this a habit."

"I can't promise you that. Gift giving is my love language. When I see a need or desire in those I care about, it's theirs. You, my friend, need some self-care, relaxation, and a little retail therapy."

"A little?" She held up a handful of gift cards. "Mr. Landry, this isn't a little of anything."

I laughed at the new knowledge I gained from this conversation. "I see you hate compliments *and* gifts. We will have to change that. You're not getting rid of me, woman. Learn to accept what I give, or I will do more."

Khaliyah narrowed her eyes at me, but my stance challenged her. "I can't with you, Airen."

You can and you will. Soon enough.

TWENTY-THREE

Airen

"I'M so proud of you, nephew. It took a woman to make yo' ass go outside." Unc patted my back. I heard you two had quite the New Year's celebration while we were in Vegas.

I nodded my head at the blow, but also at the accuracy. It wasn't about letting my guard down because of a woman. Khaliyah made me forget about the world. Luckily, those fears I'd stored up were all in my head.

"We did. It was a family affair. The entire weekend felt like a dream."

The six of us went downtown and enjoyed many of the festivities Houston had to offer this time of year. We even drove to Galveston to see Christmas lights at Moody Gardens. It felt so...normal.

"I bet it did." Unc sat next to me while Aunt Maya and Ariyah made cookies and popcorn for our last-minute movie night. "I hope you've learned that the world is not waiting on you to step outside into their territory only to get all up in your business like before. Let's call a spade a spade. The people in your life were the ones those blogs were after. Unfortunately, some people made a fortune from your personal life."

"Unc, please. I don't even want to talk about her."

"I know you don't. All I will say is that she misses you."

"All I will say is, oh the fuck well. She did what she did and got what she got. I'm not changing my mind."

"Airen, she's your—"

"Daddy! Aubrey's here!" Ariyah jumped up and down at the front door.

I didn't know Khaliyah was coming. My face must have shown my thoughts, because Uncle Rochon winked at me. He walked to the door and opened it before anyone knocked.

"Hey, my beautiful niece!" Unc picked Aubrey up and covered her face with kisses. She giggled along with him.

Aubrey's regard landed on Ariyah, and she squealed in Unc's face. "Ariyah!"

"Well, I guess that means you're done with me." He bent over to put her down, but she hugged him again and ran to my daughter. The thought of them being stepsisters wasn't a bad one.

"Whuddup, nephews!" Unc dapped each of Khaliyah's sons up before they crossed the threshold. Another thought of wanting sons crossed my mind.

Khaliyah came with everything I wanted—a large family with two boys and two girls. I could have it all if things went our way. Plus, I wouldn't have to start all over with diapers and late nights. I wanted Khaliyah to be mine. The desire to be the provider and protector of our entire family together gave me chills. God had a plan.

Not that I doubted you, God. I didn't think about this route to getting it. Thank you in advance. I see it now.

Ashtyn and Aydyn were surprisingly happy to see me. This time, not because of my stats, but because of the quality time we spent with each other as a family. Those two were fun and funny. Khaliyah acted embarrassed when they didn't hold back. I had to help her relax with all the corrections. I enjoyed the black boy joy in all of its glory. Her boys were silly as hell.

After they released me from their bear hugs, I finally laid

eyes on the woman I now knew was from my dreams. Not the nightmares I'd had with Mercy and her. Just the woman who checked off all of my boxes when I made a declaration with God. I'd only consider loving again if she existed. She stood before me, wearing a contagious smile.

"Hey, you!" she greeted as I walked toward her.

I opened my arms for her to meet me halfway. "Hey, back at you."

Her scent filled my nostrils, making me hold her tighter. Every single time we embraced, I didn't want to let her go.

Forgetting we weren't alone, the sound of Aunt Maya's throat clearing brought me back to real time. "Didn't y'all just see each other?"

Khaliyah snapped back. "Don't I hug you when I see you? Day after day after da—"

"If you hugged me that long, I'd think you were in love with me, child," she stated, wearing a grin that made me laugh.

"Oop, now you're being messy." She smiled and held her aunt in her arms as long as we did. "I'm so in love now."

Aunt Maya laughed. "You ain't funny. Come help us finish these snacks. Men and young men, please get the pillows and blankets and make sure we have enough seats."

"But I thought we were going bowling, Uncle Rochon," Ashtyn complained, which looked like news to Khaliyah.

She looked back at Unc and said, "Um, I was told this was a movie night."

Aunt Maya interjected, "It is, but if they had different plans, it's fine. You and Airen can stay with me and the girls."

"Or the two of you can take the boys. It's whatever y'all want," Unc added.

Khaliyah put her hand on her hip. "What are y'all up to?"

Unc raised his hands in the air. "I'm only trying to be accommodating, Liyah."

Khaliyah's eyes flew toward me. "Isn't that against your

being out and about policy?" she whispered. "We'd be kinda stationary. People could get a good look at you."

I leaned down a bit to whisper back, "It's cool with me if it's cool with you. I'm not hiding anymore."

Her head tilted to the side with a little smirk. "Okay, incog-negro really finna be out in these streets!"

"Nah, none of that. Only hanging with the fam," I corrected her.

"The fam," Aunt Maya repeated. "I like the sound of that."

Me too.

Khaliyah rolled her eyes. "Of course you do. Y'all ain't slick."

"Slicker than them damn edges," Aunt Maya came back with a quickness. The boys instigated with their "ooohs."

"Y'all can ooh y'all asses back to the car and back home."

Ashtyn straightened up immediately. "Ma, please. I wanna go bowling. We gotta prove we can beat you even worse than on the *Wii*." Of all my new games, they chose the original *Wii*. They played it the most.

"A'ight, now we have to go. These boys can't keep thinking they're hot stuff. Live bowling is a whole different ball game. A lesson needs to be taught, and I'm the perfect one to humble both of you," I stated with all the confidence in the world. These boys were not ready for this ass whooping but I'd happily give it.

"I'm saying. Cocky ain't cute, but you 'bout to learn today. Let's go," Khaliyah added.

"Yes!" Aydyn whispered to no one.

THE CAR RIDE WAS QUIET. Ashtyn and Aydyn didn't take their loss well. Neither of them bowled over a hundred.

Khaliyah getting in their faces after each bad bowl didn't make it any better. She wasn't the kind of mom who let her kids win. I loved that.

"Y'all hungry?" I asked to put some words in the silent space.

"After that beat-down, they should be." Khaliyah rubbed in. After the boys kissed their teeth loudly, she snickered. "Okay, okay. I'm sorry. I love you."

"Love you, too," they said at the same time with the same low energy.

I tried not to laugh, but their puppy-dog faces were hilarious. They did not back up all their trash-talking this time, so I wanted to buy them dinner, at least.

"I know a place we can get some good sandwiches not too far from here," I suggested.

"Sandwiches? We don't eat out for sandwiches," Ashtyn answered.

Khaliyah chuckled at her son's bitter voice. She looked at me and mouthed, "Poor baby."

"Trust me, you'll like it. They got something for everybody. My homeboy and his wife own the place."

"I'm good with it," Aydyn said.

Ashtyn kept his gaze out the window. "I can't make no promises, but I'll try."

"Sound more excited," Khaliyah demanded. "A football star is offering you a meal out and about." Her goofy behind giggled.

"Maaannn, he wasn't supposed to be that good on the lanes, too." Ashtyn crossed his arms across his chest. I glanced back at them way too much in the rearview mirror. I almost felt bad. Almost.

We made our way to O.C. BBQ, and no one recognized me. I felt stupid for staying inside the last two years to avoid absolutely nothing.

"Good evening, Kalie!" I greeted the young woman behind the counter.

"Uncle!" she said a little too loudly. Her mouth opened wide before it turned into a smile. "You're not eating in the back?" she whispered.

"Not today. I have my people with me, so we will dine up front," I proudly proclaimed.

Her smile warmed my heart. Victor set a damn good example for me regarding a blended family. Kalie looked at Khaliyah and the boys. "Is this the lady I heard Daddy talking about?" She outed me.

I put my finger up to my lips, but not quickly enough.

"Uhh, what now?" Khaliyah asked playfully. "What was said?"

"All good things," Kalie answered truthfully, but she didn't take the hint and stop there. "Daddy said we'd possibly have an addition to our extended family if Uncle Airen played his cards right."

"Woooowww, Kalie," was all I could say.

Everyone laughed, including the boys.

"I'm sorry. Sort of." Kalie scrunched her face at me. "What can I get you?"

"So, this is their first time," I informed her. "I need to make them believers. You give us what you think is best."

"Bet," she said as she tapped away on the screen. Kalie told me the total. After I tapped my card, she gave me my receipt. "It will be out shortly."

I suddenly remembered I had manners. Not like they mattered now. "By the way, Khaliyah, Ashtyn, and Aydyn, this is Kalie. She's Victor's daughter and part-time employee."

"We're also neighbors," Kalie threw out there. "I've seen y'all from a distance before."

I lowered my head. "Kalie, you gotta keep some things to yourself. You sound like a stalker."

"What?" She shrugged with no shame. "My window faces the street. I look outside now and then. More often than not, I witness my neighbors and their frequent visitors. Most Saturdays in the past few months, to be exact. I can't help it if I like natural light."

"You like being nosy," I shot at her.

We laughed before I walked us to a vacant booth.

"So, you talk about my mom to your friends?" Ashtyn rubbed his hands together like a secret plan was coming together.

Khaliyah and I met eyes with the same sentiment—these kids.

TWENTY-FOUR

Khaliyah

I'D MADE the biggest mistake of my days recently and granted my ex-husband a quick lunch. He apparently had a meeting in Houston and took the short flight. His returning flight would leave before the kids were out of school.

As much as I'd like to avoid him for the rest of my life, we shared three things in common, and there was no way around it. Even though I didn't agree with everything he did as a father, I gave him courtesy as the man I created my original family with.

I came here expecting him to apologize for his behavior at our sons' party. It'd been a month with no word. As parents, we needed to get things straight and be clear about certain boundaries. He'd crossed many that night.

Christian greeted me at the table when I finally made it. My prayers in the car have already calmed my nerves on the drive over. I approached everything with love, reflecting my life's goals. I no longer allowed my emotions to fluctuate when they didn't have to. Any time in his presence was temporary. I'd focus on that fact.

The purpose of this lunch finally made its appearance. The new Mrs. Luke wanted to spend more quality time with her step-children and possibly do a family shoot with the five of them. It came out too fast for me to catch my burst of laughter. I hadn't seen the woman since she disrespectfully walked into the home my children and I had occupied. Then she crashed their party with this fool. No one had shown courtesy in handling things, and I'd forgiven them both. However, forgiveness created a radar to detect any similar recurring behaviors.

"Come on, Khaliyah! Help me out with this one. It will mean a lot to her."

I raised a finger to my mouth to ensure my following words didn't seem like an attack, but the question had to be asked. "Does she know you gave up all of your parental rights? You didn't fight for custody or anything."

"That was a mistake on my part. I was hurt. You let me down." I jerked my head but reeled it back. His perception and experience mattered. *Don't take it personally, Khaliyah.* "Look. We had some good times. We really did, but I couldn't get over how much you ignored my needs. I did everything I could for us. You didn't reciprocate.

"If that is how you remember it, that's cool."

Quick to listen, slow to speak, slow to anger. I repeated the verse over and over in my head as I'd done while married to this man. Only God knew how I endured without losing my mind.

"Stop acting like you didn't have it good. I paid for everything you wanted and needed. The kids wanted for nothing. You have your family thinking I abandoned you and my kids with your distorted memory."

"My recollection is just fine, which is why I'm leaving. You are a piece of work, and I no longer have to grin and bear it. My answer is no. Goodbye, Christian."

"So, you're just walking out on me like that? After all I've done for you. I gave you a good life. Now you can't even listen to my side of things during another meal *I'm* paying for. You're being unbelievably ungrateful."

Everything I wanted to say before no longer mattered. I was done. I stood, then leaned toward him so only he could hear me. "Christian, thank you! Thank you for the handful of memories in a sea of misery with you. Thank you for our children. Fuck you for everything else."

"Khaliyah," he called after me as I walked my ungrateful ass away from him. "Khaliyah," he yelled again when I reached the door.

"STOP!" was all my mind yelled. *If not now, then when?*

I exhaled to let all of my anger leave my body so I could do what needed to be done. I returned to the table where Christian sat, smirking as if I'd come back because he requested it.

"That's what I—"

I raised my hand to stop him. "Before I walk away today, you need to understand something."

"Hell, no. That's not how this works. Your bitter ass wanna use my kids to get to me."

"How so, Christian?" I rested my chin on my fist. "I want to hear this."

"Don't be a smart ass, Khaliyah."

"Don't be an asshole. You can't help it, so say what you gotta say."

He tightened his eyes and continued with his pointless point. "My lady wants to take some innocent family pictures. I am their father; the least you can do is accommodate me after taking my kids and running to another city." I nodded as I took in everything that came out of his mouth. "I ain't say nothing about that nigga you got hanging around them. I'd do my research about him if I were you. His last wife didn't—"

"Christian, that's enough. Let's break this all the way down so it never has to be spoken of again. First, I'm not bitter. You walked away from us, and we are better for it. Trust! Second, your audacity coming at me like this is wild. You act like I owe you something when it comes to my kids. *My* kids. The same ones you did not need, since they would forever be under my influence." He rolled his eyes and kissed his teeth. "Nah, boo. Those were your exact fucking words. Being the type of woman I am, I never stopped you from seeing my kids. I encouraged it so they wouldn't grow up thinking their father didn't love them."

"How dare—"

"I'm not done. Your intentions are no longer my concern. Your actions weren't shy when they spoke on your behalf. You will not use my children to make yourself look like a good father. You aren't." His head jerked as if I had hit him in the face. "Look stupid all you want. Living in the same house as your kids is not being there for them. Going to work every day does not qualify you as a good husband and father, either."

"Khaliyah," he interrupted me.

I lifted my hand again. "Still going. I will no longer allow you around my children, since you don't seem to understand why we are where we are. You show up when you want, how you want. You think paying bills excuses your bullshit for all those years? You were the best example of what my sons never want to be.

"I taught them how to use the restroom like a man. I teach them every day about responsibility and accountability. I show up for them the way they need me to. You had all the time in the world to do so when you had us.

"We are no longer under your thumb or roof. You are not responsible for us. You can keep every single dime you give if that keeps you over there with your wife. Start a new life and act like you don't know us. You did it so well when we lived in the same house. Keep up the poor work and leave us the hell alone."

"You really gonna sit in my face and tell me I wasn't there for my kids?"

"Sure the hell did. The truth can be painful when you open your damn eyes. We're the happiest we've ever been. That speaks volumes about your absence. So, thank you for doing what I couldn't. You filed for divorce, and now you have it. You gave up your rights; we will now act like it. I won't ask you for anything. You are responsible for your relationship with my kids. If they choose to have one with you, that will be their decision. I hope you have a nice life because we sure will. You did us all a favor. Keep it up. And since I'm done, I'll say one more fuck you for the road. Goodbye, Mr. Luke."

Sometimes, curiosity got the best of me. Today was exactly that. I wanted to see if he'd changed—not for me, but for our children. If Christian shed his normal selfish skin, he could have a better relationship with them. My kids never ask about him.

I beat myself up for thinking this would be anything other than what it was. He'd moved on and seemed happy on the outside, but he was the same. Maya Angelou told me how to handle people like him, but dammit if I didn't constantly recreate hope of him growing the fuck up.

"When someone shows you who they are, believe them the first time."

I'm a believer now.

AFTER HANDING my frustrations to God for about an hour, I let them go before the kids got home. Christian broke my heart year after year. I was happy to get all of that off my chest, but it didn't erase my pain or my memories. I'd prayed for God to remove it all, but I wasn't stupid. I understood that the painful process wasn't entirely over.

My energy had to be good for the night we had planned. Another Friday with Airen and Ariyah. This time, I needed to be in their presence—in Airen's presence. Although we were only friends, he made things feel so right.

The night flew by like a freight train. We ate, played, showered, watched a movie, ate again, and then the kids dispersed. The boys took over Airen's game room while the girls played in Ariyah's room.

It gave me and Airen some time to talk over wine. Airen was a family man. Children were always a dream of his. He claimed he missed the opportunity to have more and regretted it. He was an amazing dad. I witnessed that with my own eyes. My aunt loved him like a son, which also spoke volumes. She never liked Christian.

We put the kids to bed an hour ago. Before we'd go our separate ways, Airen gave me the alarm code to the house.

"You trust me like that?" I asked.

"Maybe." He slightly shrugged with that sexy ass smirk. "I don't want you to feel trapped in if you need to step out. Plus, I can easily change it when you leave."

"Thanks for the confidence."

"What?"

"Nothing. I know I wouldn't do anything crazy, but I understand what you're saying. With your low-key, under-the-radar vibe in the outside world, trusting people has to be an issue."

"Yeah, it is. People aren't always genuine. Some of these muthafuckas are superb actors. Not talking about you. I have to do everything with caution. Ariyah is my everything. I have to protect her. This fucked up world created many fucked up people."

"You're preaching to the choir. One day, you think you have a future with someone who wouldn't dream of hurting you, and the next, you find out that's their intention with every new day. It's fucked up for real. I wish people would show both faces and give us a chance to choose if we wanna be around for it all."

"Seems like we met the same type of folks."

"I wouldn't know. You don't really share that side of you."

He chuckled. "Touché. It's hard to talk about. We'll have that conversation one day."

"Well, I'm gonna get some sleep. I'll see you in the morning."

"Goodnight, Khaliyah."

I left Airen behind in the kitchen. There was a pain in that man I couldn't put my finger on. A simple Google search could cure my curiosity, but it seemed like cheating. He shared his hatred for gossip blogs and the mess they caused for his family. His name would for sure come up with truth and lies. I'd rather learn it from his mouth.

After poking my head into Ariyah's room and finding Aubrey knocked out on one side of the bed. Ariyah stirred a bit, so I quietly closed the door. I didn't want to be the reason her rest got interrupted.

I turned on the balls of my feet to head down the hall and check on the boys when a whisper of my name almost prematurely separated my soul from my flesh.

"Why? Airen!" I whisper-yelled. My skin crawled, itching every inch. "Why?"

"I'm so sorry," finally exited his mouth once he stood up from quietly cracking up. "I didn't know you'd be so jumpy. I'm sorry."

He met me in the middle of the hall. "You're wrong for laughing that hard. I'm a guest, punk ass."

"I promise I'm sorry, but..." His barely silent chuckles made me laugh at myself. Ain't no way I didn't make some ugly ass face. I was an easy target to sneak up on.

"I didn't hear you come upstairs," I admitted.

"I check on Ariyah to make sure she's good."

"Yeah, I do the same with my kids."

Airen peeked into his daughter's room. He exhaled with a smile. "She looks so peaceful." He closed the door. "Ari's been having bizarre nightmares. Looks like I'll actually get to sleep alone throughout the night."

Don't judge me, but part of me was disappointed that he didn't finish the sentence with an "unless…" We both knew it wasn't going down, but I still wanted to hear it.

"Well, goodnight. One 'mo 'gain." I turned toward the boys' room and made sure they weren't still up. I caught the usual snores from them both. Satisfied with my babies' safety and comfort, I retreated to my room. Airen had already left the hall.

I closed the door to my room and really took the place in. Who had king-size beds in guest rooms? An ex-football player, I guess. I remembered Izak and Nick, and it made sense. When they visited, they sometimes slept here.

Someone must have manufactured this mattress in heaven. How was it so soft, but the perfect amount of firmness? I spent money on my bed; it didn't feel this good. I fell back on the pillow to get the total experience. This damn bed wrapped its arms around me. I didn't care how crazy it sounded.

I closed my eyes for a second. My heart felt like it'd burst. An alarm sounded. It took a moment to gather my mind. My phone.

Amber alert.

I kept telling myself to disable the notification, then I'd think about if it was my kid. I glanced at the notification of the description of a mother who took her kids after not showing up at a court custody hearing yesterday afternoon. Those kids were most likely safe. I still said a prayer for the family.

It was only 2:12 a.m. My mind conjured up Christian.

Ashtyn reminded me regularly, "He gave up his rights." Our earlier encounter reiterated that fact.

Closing my eyes only took me to the day we left the house. I couldn't shake the feeling of wishing I fucked up his now wife for that stunt. Sleep left the room for the time being. I was so glad Airen gave me the alarm code.

TWENTY-FIVE

Khaliyah

I SNUCK DOWNSTAIRS and entered the code near the garage door. After a few beeps, I waited to make sure no one woke up. After the coast was clear, I proceeded to the backyard. The bench swing had my name on it.

The middle-of-the-night temperature wasn't too bad. I rested my body on the bench and rocked myself into a daze. Hypothetical nonsense flooded my mind, playing out the many ways all of this could lead to. The best possible scenario was that I had gained a genuine friend.

Another had my mind beyond the gutter. I tried to shake it off because ain't no way this man didn't have a plethora of females on call when he needed to relieve some stress. My dreams had already been invaded for months. Sleeping in this man's house didn't make it any easier.

I breathed out to clear my mind of Airen and tried to contemplate what I had planned for work next week. The mental notes were coming in when I heard the door open.

"You good?" Airen asked, poking his head outside.

"Yes. I didn't mean to wake you. I couldn't sleep and figured the night air would help."

He stepped outside, making his way to me. "You didn't wake me."

"I should be the one asking you if you're good. It's late, mister."

He smiled. "No shit." After stopping in front of me, he tapped my legs. "Lemme sit next to you. You can rest your legs on me."

"Um, I'll keep my feet on my side."

"Khaliyah, you can stretch out. I'm not gonna judge your stinky feet."

"Negro, my feet don't stink."

"That's what all women say."

"I bet you'd know." I winced at the sound of my own words. No way to take it back now.

The man faced me halfway. "What's that supposed to mean?"

"Nothing. I'm tired. Don't pay me any mind."

"Khaliyah, you couldn't pay me not to pay you any mind. Trust me."

Now, what's *that* supposed to mean?'

Airen pulled my legs toward him, forcing me to rest them on his thighs. "As far as your assumption. I don't know a lot of women in general or personally."

I badly wanted to defend myself and lie about the intent behind my words, but he caught it.

He released a long sigh. "We're friends, right?" He asked. "Good enough that I can talk to you about something on my mind?"

I shrugged. "Sure."

"Cool. So...a woman has caught my eye."

My heart sank. I mean, I wasn't looking for a man at all. Not now anyway. Something about Airen made me want to reserve a place for him. I wanted him to be the man I never realized I desired. Here he was, putting me deep in the friend zone, about to tell me about another woman.

Christian said I wasn't wife material since I failed as a team player. His dumb ass called me a glorified babysitter and it never actually hit me until now. Maybe he was right. Perhaps that's how men viewed me—a potential burden. Before I spiraled any further, I jumped back into the present.

"Oh, yeah?" I played along, ignoring the pain of my crushed fantasies.

"She's beautiful, successful, sexy without an ounce of effort." My thoughts traveled to Kaitlyn. I'd bet she'd be his type. I hated the bitch, but I wasn't blind.

Airen continued as he stared at the pool. "It's a bit intimidating since I promised not to get into another relationship again. After my wife died, I vowed I was done with love. I wanted to focus on raising my daughter. However, this woman got me rethinking everything, and I haven't even told her I like her."

I swallowed hard, exhaled slowly to make sure my jealousy and disappointment didn't show on my sleeve. The conversation at the park crossed my mind. He made me believe we were feeling each other. Now this?

Maybe he'd already dismissed the possibility of us. We'd spent enough time together to recognize what the other had to offer. As embarrassing as it was, I played it off and gave him advice as a friend. "I'm all for honesty. If it could be something, say something. Love is a risk either way, but you'd probably regret letting her slip away, especially if there's potential for her to be the one for you. I'd love to find that one day. But a bad experience can spoil you on the idea."

Airen pressed his lips together hard. "Khaliyah, you'd be the perfect piece to any good man's life."

"I don't know about all of that. I come with not one but three kids. It's kind of already written off for me. I couldn't even bring myself to ask a man to take us on." Especially if that man wasn't Airen.

He nudged my arm with his elbow. "The right one would."

"Yeah, if God ever created him." I chuckled softly. I need us to finish this conversation ASAP. "So, about this woman, tell her the whole truth. Be real about your reservations and the reasons behind them. Make her aware that you're prepared to adjust your viewpoint for her."

"Sounds easy, but how would I even start that conversation? She's guarded, too."

I chuckled at the idea of talking to my sons someday about expressing interest in a girl. Airen didn't seem like one who needed any advice. Then again, he had a kind heart. I liked that about him. Whoever this woman was would benefit from it.

"Say you like her and go from there."

"Cool." He nodded with confidence. "I can do that."

Airen's legs stretched forth as he began pushing the swing back. I tried to steal a glimpse of his face. Being a friend probably wouldn't be that bad.

"So, Khaliyah, I gotta admit something."

My shoulders tensed, expecting another emotional blow. "What's up?"

"I like you," came out of his mouth.

I burst out laughing, and so did he. "Airen, please tell me you're joking. You were talking about me?" I asked, completely relieved and feeling like a dummy.

Airen's closed-lipped smile eased my spirit. "Woman, you came up in here with a hold on me that got me renegotiating everything I promised myself. I don't know if I like it. Nobody's ever done that before."

The giggles came over me out of nowhere. "You sound like me. I like you, too. I don't like how much I like you. You came out of nowhere."

"Nah, that's all you. I've been here."

"So competitive. I'll let you have it."

"Damn, you tryna give it to me already." He tugged at my shirt.

"Get slapped. You ain't getting nothing from me that easy. It's bad enough that I'm conceding to my no-relationships rule. I got two questions."

Airen exhaled like an elephant stood up from his chest and finally let him be. "Okay." His eyes met mine, ready for me to ask away.

"You think I'm guarded?"

"Khaliyah, stop playing. You shut down anything too deep. It's like you don't want me to see you."

"It's because I don't want to be hurt again. I got a whole ass family, which brings me to my second question. You know I got kids, right? Like I got a lotta them."

It was his turn to burst out laughing. "Yeah, I noticed. I've always desired a large family. It doesn't matter how they come into my life. That's God's work."

"Okay. Let's say we dated, and it turned into something serious. We are a lot."

"Stop trying to convince me you're not worth it. You have good kids. I enjoy having y'all here. It's weird when y'all leave. Quieter. Not in a good way."

"You're serious?"

"I am."

"Okay. How does this work? What's next?"

"Well, first off, we need some playdates without kids." He tapped his chin with his index finger as if in deep thought. "I remember people calling them dates. It's been so long."

"You're silly."

"Sometimes." He rubbed my legs. "What do you say? Can I take you on a date?"

"I'd love that."

TWENTY-SIX

Airen

A DATE.

Khaliyah agreed to let me take her on a date. My last date was probably when Mercy was pregnant with Ari. Life went all the way left afterward. Going out with a woman to learn about her, potentially to love her one day, was the top of my never-again list. Here we were.

God, I guess you are cracking up at my list, especially knowing who you had in store for me.

Khaliyah was different. Every man who found the right one probably thought the same thing when they met their lady. Months ago, I would've laughed in each man's face, considering them all damn fools. I fell for Mercy in high school because she was different, too. Still, there was no comparison of how I felt as a horny teen to the way I felt right now about a woman with three children—an established family in which I'd have to make my mark.

I chuckled at the memory of believing I had everything correctly planned out. How wrong was I?

I'll take your plans over mine each and every time, Father.

After being completely done getting ready except for my feet, I sat on my bed, where Ariyah had been waiting and watching me for the last fifteen minutes. "You have to tell her she's pretty, Daddy," my daughter offered her advice. How a five-year-old believed she had anything to teach me about dating was beyond me.

"That should be easy since it's true." I winked at her as I put my socks on.

Maya was coming over since Unc had his friends at the house. Our first date fell on the perfect Saturday. We were going to an escape room, a drive-in movie, and then dinner. "Nothing fancy," played in my head in Khaliyah's voice. She let me make the plans, but told me everything she didn't want to do.

Khaliyah was everything I never thought of asking God for the first time around. Knowing I had deep pockets didn't cause her to make expensive plans. She wanted me. To know me. Not Airen Landry. Just Airen.

"Guess what?" Ariyah said, with the biggest, most beautiful smile.

"What?" I stood and walked out of my room with her on my tail.

"I love you."

I stopped in my tracks, and my baby girl ran into me. I turned around and picked her up. "I love you more. You will always be my number one girl." Sprinkling pecks all over her cheeks and forehead, she giggled before hugging me tightly.

"My dream came true, Daddy."

We both pulled back to see one another better. "Yeah? Which one?"

Ariyah's lips stretched wide, exposing her baby teeth. "Miss Khaliyah being my new mommy."

As much as I wanted to be realistic with her, I agreed in spirit that her dream was, in fact, becoming our reality day by day. I was aware and wouldn't pretend otherwise. I asked,

"How does that make you feel?" Her infectious joy revealed the answer to my question, but I wanted to hear it in her words.

Ariyah blushed before opening her mouth to say, "Happy, Daddy. Very happy." She snickered. "You know why?"

I put her down, and we sat on the top step. "Why?"

"Aunt Maya said Aubrey will be my sister! I really want a sister. And I will have two brothers." She basically yelled the "two" part. "Then I won't be by myself no more. I will have a lot of family."

"You would. That's four more people in the house. Can you handle that?"

"Yes, Daddy!" she said matter-of-factly. "I want them here all the time. Aunt Maya told me to wait until you stop being hardheaded with your heart."

I shook my head, making sure I heard her right. "Aunt Maya said that?"

"She says it aaalllll the time," Ariyah dragged her voice. "She always say…" she stopped and got into character with her hand on her hip, mimicking her great aunt. "He's so hardheaded with his heart. Just so hardheaded with his heart." Ariyah raised her hands in the air. "What even does that mean, Daddy?"

"It means your aunt talks too much." I tickled her. Aunt Maya was really out here talking about me to my five-year-old. Damn.

Right on cue, the doorbell rang. Ariyah ran down the stairs toward our home's entrance. I followed closely behind her. "She's here!" I let her aunt in, and before I could tell her about herself, Ariyah took my hand and pulled me toward the garage. "Now you can go date Miss Khaliyah."

Maya and I laughed at this girl trying to push me out of the house. In her mind, the sooner, the better.

"Um, RiRi?" Aunt Maya called out. Ariyah stopped manhandling me and gave her attention to Maya. "Shouldn't your dad wear shoes? He may possibly need his wallet, keys, and things before you kick him out."

"What your aunt said. We all know Daddy has been so hardheaded with his heart, so I'm gonna go." I looked directly at Maya when it came out of my mouth. Her face gave me every piece of evidence I needed.

Ariyah took off toward my room. It happened so fast that I didn't get to tell her that my shoes were by the couch, a few feet away from me. I wanted to talk to Maya alone, anyway.

My uncle's wife looked at me and pressed her lips out to the side, standing her ground. "We shole do! I'm glad you finally recognize the truth and are doing something about it."

I narrowed my eyes at her, annoyed at her being right. My first instinct was to argue my point, but there was no use. Her observation about my heart was spot on. I didn't want to use it anymore. I was hardheaded. She and Uncle Rochon have said it for the past couple of years. Mercy had been gone for three, and we were done long before she left for good.

"I am. Not sure if Ari is getting siblings and a mother out of it. Cuz somebody is putting things in her head."

"Boy, I ain't did nothing but speak the truth. RiRi knows it too. That's why she keeps having dreams about it. How would you explain her dream before you met Khaliyah?"

"Maya, she's five. She will believe you. What if Khaliyah doesn't see me that way after we date?"

"How about you try accepting what I say? You and my niece are both hardheaded with your hearts. If you'd let your guards down, you'd see how good you are for each other. Those boys adore you. The girls are already sisters, if you ask me. The kids are ready, in my opinion. They are waiting for their parents to stop lying to themselves."

I had nothing. Admitting she was right and that I'd come to the same realization was more than I was willing to do. Ariyah broke the pause between us, dropping a trail of shoes behind her. "I couldn't pick one." She put down the pile of shoes in front of me.

"Thank you, big girl. I'll pick a pair and get on with my date."

"Yay!" She jumped in a circle around me.

"Are you going with a gift? Nothing big. Anything to say you thought about her."

"Yeah, I'm stopping at the flower shop on the way. It's paid for and waiting for me."

"Good man! Well, we don't want you to be late. Show my baby a good time. I already know you're the one for her, and she's the one for you." She caught the movement before I could follow through. "Aht! I know you don't believe in soul-mates. I'm saying she's the one worth experiencing this life-time with. Y'all need to take advantage of this second chance. Prove it to yourselves, and we can all move forward as a big, happy family."

<hr>

I PULLED up at Khaliyah's after picking up her bouquet. I was a confident man any day and every day. I knew who I was and stayed true to my values, even when it meant letting go of my first wife.

What I was experiencing was different.

Different was the weakest word in the dictionary to describe the woman. Khaliyah was breathtaking, but also satis-fying. She fulfilled needs and expectations that were not there until I laid eyes on her. The woman had an aura that snatched my attention and heart from day one, almost like she'd been waiting on me for some time.

One of the first things Ariyah said after she'd spent time with Khaliyah played in my head. "I want you to be my new mommy." With no hesitation, no doubt. Even my daughter knew what she wanted and had no problem speaking her truth.

My reserve had nothing to do with Khaliyah as a woman. It had everything to do with my experience with women. There were a few who broke my heart, and trusting another one seemed close to impossible. Yet, here we were.

Trust.

I trusted Khaliyah with everything—even my daughter. I'd make excuses about keeping the playdates at my house and in my presence so I could spend time with Aubrey's mother. Learning as much as I had hours at a time sank me deeper into my need for her. Being near was all I wanted. Playing it off around my family became a job. I didn't want to hear the "I told you so" from everyone who promised me that God would send me the right woman to right all the wrongs in my life. Most of all, my mindset regarding love was wrong.

Genuine love.

An unconditional love where no circumstance and no one could squeeze in even an ounce of doubt.

Since my uncle's party, I was the one who put doubt in my mind to protect my heart. Trusting the wrong person would not only affect me. My daughter's well-being was my responsibility. Khaliyah's love for her children and even Ariyah at this point gave me all the assurance I needed to dispel my own lies.

Whenever I got too comfortable with the idea, I'd conjure a ridiculous what-if. I couldn't accept that the woman who'd changed my love view came to me with no effort on my part. It made little sense to me. I didn't have to go looking for her. She walked into my life because my daughter found a friend in hers.

I felt...undeserving.

I shook my reservations away and nodded to everything right about this. Us. Our family. The pull. The dreams. My daughter's desires. Shit, my desires. The heavenly ones and the unholy ones. This was the first step to getting it all.

I was ready.

TWENTY-SEVEN

Khaliyah

"So, you really done bagged you a fine ass, rich ass, football player?" Karina sat on my bed, watching me change into another outfit.

I rolled my eyes at her words. "I didn't bag anyone. We like each other and are going on one date."

She kissed her teeth. "Then another and another. Then, there will be a ring, a wedding, perhaps a baby or two, and happily ever after. Just like all of my favorite books."

"Tuh! Your favorite books always have something to do with a criminal snagging an innocent woman who becomes so infatuated that his criminal ways become hers. We ain't that. Especially those extra babies you tried to throw in there."

Karina shrugged. "Same difference. Airen's a man who lived in the spotlight and was the talk of every sports network and blog. Something you'd never pay attention to. Now, you're about to get married again. If anybody can knock you up, it's him. The nigga is fine. I remember his ass on magazine covers."

"Slow your roll, Cole." We laughed. "One date." I stared at myself in the full-length mirror.

My mind drifted off into another life where I met him first; the babies from me were his. Neither of us would have experienced the type of heartbreak we'd had. The right one from the start. Why couldn't it have been that way?

I dropped my head and smiled at the thought of him being the right one. Not someone perfect, but worth going through life with. Willing to have each other's backs and battle whatever came our way together. That type of right. No second-guessing even when we're at odds.

Karina's face let me know she noticed my drift, and I would hear her mouth about it. "You like him." She smiled big and wide. "I see it when you talk about him. Shit, even when you think of him." The woman's squeal caused my cheeks to warm.

"Like you said, you've seen him. It's probably lust. It's been a long time since a man has been interested in me."

"Lies! It's been a long time since you've been interested in anyone."

I poked my lips to the side. She had a point. Airen was the exception. Our daughters gave us no choice but to get to know each other enough to get to this point. Still, it was seriously one date.

"Maybe."

"Mr. Airen must be offering something your heart can't refuse because I have watched you shut down every man who looked your way. Even ones on his level of fine." She put her hand up to stop me from protesting. "You don't have to say anything. I am happy for you. Happy that you at least found someone worth your time. These men out here can be full of shit. We both have more experience with that truth than we should. I am proud of you. Letting your guard down wasn't easy."

"Thank you, boo. I didn't plan on being so guarded. I was tired. Airen didn't try anything when we met. The time we've spent together gave me a glimpse of him as a father and a man before I knew about the football part."

"God knew you would never have given that man a chance if you did."

We laughed out loud. She understood all too well how true that was. A sports superstar meant fame and people in your business. According to my aunt, his name went through the mud at the height of his career.

"Wear that!" She pointed out the black jeans I jumped and wriggled into. "Put the white shirt back on with my jacket."

"Okay. What about the shoes?" I asked. We walked into my closet, and I tried on about four pairs before Karina chose one.

She made life considerably better. Although we were only three hours away all those years, it required planning to see each other. Our daily phone calls worked mostly, but I missed her so much.

I got fully dressed minus the shoes, and we settled in the kitchen for a couple of shots. My nerves got the best of me. I knew I was a good woman, but that meant nothing when my insecurity poked her damn head into my thoughts.

Airen's outer appearance alone would attract any model, actress, athlete, you name it, who loved a chocolate, carved-to-perfection exterior. His heart and mind were the icing on the cake for most. For me, it was the first thing that made this step possible. Looks got too much credit in my immature mind when I was younger.

I was choosing for more than a good time. I was choosing for compatibility, unconditional friendship, and love. I had to choose for my kids. If they had their way, we'd be living with Airen already. They never wanted to leave his house, and he was all my boys talked about since they met him.

Karina left me to my thoughts when I got the call that Airen was on the way. Airen Landry showed up out of nowhere, but had been around forever. My aunt married Rochon over a decade ago. I remembered her mentioning her new man, who had a nephew who played football. They traveled the country for his games. It meant absolutely nothing to me. Being married with two small kids had me quite occupied, and I abhorred sports. Thanks to my ex-husband.

A knock at my door sped my ticker into overdrive. I took as much air in as I could and released it slowly.

It's simply a date, Khaliyah.

I opened the door to the most gorgeous specimen of a man I'd ever seen, holding a bouquet of pink roses. My smile damn near broke my face and brought one to his.

"Hello, Miss Khaliyah."

"Airen." I moved to the side so he could come inside.

Jesus! His cologne tapped the bad side of my shoulder as he walked past me. It suggested that we never leave my place tonight.

Airen waited for me to close the door. He held his arms out for me. I moved my feet until my body connected to his. With the flowers in his hand, he wrapped his arms around me. Those powerful arms eased all of my anxiety like magic. The rise and fall of his chest against my cheek was like home.

Once we let go of each other, his eyes took hold of mine. Either time slowed, or we got lost in each other for a few minutes. "How was your day?" he asked before kissing my temple and stepping back.

"Good." I found a vase in one of the many cabinets I've yet to fill in my kitchen. "Hung out with my best friend after dropping the kids off with my grandparents. How about you?" After putting water in the vase, I set it on the counter and took the bouquet from him.

Airen sighed. "Kind of tough."

"Oh! Is everything okay?"

"It is now. I've been waiting for this moment since I opened my eyes this morning."

I tried my damnedest not to blush. "Boy, you ain't gotta front."

We laughed. Airen's eyes intently held onto my gaze. "I'm serious. It's been a while, and waiting today was the hardest part."

"I know what you mean," I admitted.

Those orbs were on their worst behavior. I felt exposed. Not physically. It was as though he could see my thoughts, fears, desires, and hopes all with one look. He finally broke the silence. "You are stunning."

I pulled my jacket open a little to brush off his comment. "It's only jeans and a tee."

Airen's head lowered to the side, the slits of his eyes tightened as if I'd insulted him. "You do that a lot."

"What?"

"Dodge compliments."

I bit my lip, almost mad at myself for already revealing that part of me. It was weird to be told I looked good. My family always made me believe I was beautiful, but anyone else saying it seemed like common courtesy. People say things to get reactions without actually meaning them.

"Sorry. It's a habit."

"I'll help you break it. You are breathtaking, no matter what you have on. I'm not only observing your appearance when I say these things to you."

I pressed my lips together to refrain from disagreeing. "Thank you," I accepted his words, focusing down at my hands.

Airen smiled, then chuckled. "That looked painful."

"It was."

"Come on. Let's get out of here."

TWENTY-EIGHT

Airen

I COULDN'T KEEP my thoughts clean the entire time in her presence. Alone at her house with her looking how she looked all the damn time tested my restraint. We usually had our kids or family around, so the possibility of temptation being pursued didn't exist. That energy was heavy, so I hurried us out after finding myself staring at her for too long.

Being inside of her was not my overall goal. I'd be lying if I said it wasn't a consistent thought I had to suppress. A slow pace provided the comfort of due diligence before creating another soul tie. The carnal human side of me didn't give a shit, but I wasn't losing that war. I'd conquered my temptations for this long.

Khaliyah's jeans hugged her tight enough to make a nigga jealous. At some point, I'd get to touch her everywhere, too. The subtle floral scent I'd grown to love played on my olfactory nerves. She sat in the passenger seat of my car after I held the door for her. In the few moments walking to the driver's side, I adjusted myself so she wouldn't see what her presence did to me.

During the drive to the escape room, Khaliyah shared her excitement about completing a project for one of her larger clients yesterday. The woman was a computer programmer, which went over my head. She never went into detail, but she explained the pains of meeting every design and functionality change of websites she'd built. She considered hiring an employee to ease her workload.

I admired her love for her work, no matter how difficult it became. Others would walk away because it was too much work or not worth it. She pushed through everything. Plus, she had a couple of small side hustles to work on when she became overwhelmed with her main gig. When did she ever rest?

All I could offer her was an ear and encouragement to pray about each move and trust God to show her the right moves to make. Her hesitation in taking the next step in her business was all in her fear of releasing part of her control. Delegation meant she'd have to trust someone to complete a task as well as she would. I wanted to help her, but I didn't want to overstep. Someone came to mind, but I'd see if it was a possibility before suggesting anything.

Khaliyah smiled at me once I parked at our first destination. I'd only told her when I'd pick her up and to dress comfortably. Everything would be a surprise.

"This is perfect!" Her beautiful teeth were on full display. "You just get me, huh?"

"I listen when you talk."

"And here I thought you only undressed me with your eyes when I spoke."

I failed to muffle my laugh. "I plead the fifth."

She hit my arm before laughing. "I set myself up for that one."

"Indeed. You ready?"

Khaliyah nodded with excitement. "Don't be mad at me if I fail."

"We are here to have fun, woman."

AFTER LEAVING the escape room with t-shirts of completion, we cracked up at how competitive we became. We worked together to beat the clock with time to spare. I saw another side of Khaliyah to cherish. Once she figured it out, the woman cussed out everything she felt was stupid.

The rooftop movie awarded me a kiss on the cheek. It was an innocent gesture that replayed in my mind as we took our seats after grabbing snacks and drinks. We watched *Just Wright* with one of Khaliyah's favorite actresses. I learned that Angela Bassett, Queen Latifah, Viola Davis, and Sandra Bullock were in her top ten.

Khaliyah snuggled against me in the lounge chairs as we enjoyed the movie. My beard and hat bought me the privacy I needed to have moments like these. Being out now with no one seeing me made me think I was being preserved for Khaliyah.

"That movie never gets old," she said as we exited the elevator and headed toward the valet. I noticed some double-takes, but no one approached me, which was all I wanted.

"I'm glad you think so. I'd never seen it before."

"I am not surprised. Rom-coms aren't usually a genre men prefer. You like shooting and murder movies."

"Says the woman who's seen every single episode of every *Law and Order* and spinoffs," I said with a raised brow.

"Touché"

"You probably know how to get away with any crime."

"If I did, I wouldn't admit it. Crime docs are interesting only because it's baffling that people can be so careless about human life."

"Just make sure you're never the culprit on any episode."

Khaliyah burst out laughing as my car pulled up and the

valet guy handed me the keys. I gave him a tip and opened the door for Khaliyah.

Once I sat in the driver's seat and took off, I had to gauge whether she had the energy to do anything else. "You ready to call it a night?"

"Not really."

"Good. Food and drinks?"

"Of course."

On the way to the restaurant, we discussed our top movies or shows in different genres. Funny enough, we agreed on most of them. Surprisingly, I discovered she didn't like *Grey's Anatomy*, unlike her aunt. Maya tried to force the show on both of us. We were both stubborn enough to refuse. *9-1-1*, however, we watched faithfully and planned to make it one of our shows.

Small things like watching TV together made me want her even more. It wasn't about her body.

Let me stop lying.

It wasn't *only* about her body or beauty. Spending time with Khaliyah was all my heart desired lately. Making plans to do so without a playdate helped push my agenda, a friendship above anything else. Deep down, we had to appreciate who the other was beyond the shield and scars.

I could do this forever.

In the latter half of the drive, we let the music do the talking. My '90s playlist played, and she knew every song. Sometimes she hummed, other times she opened her mouth slightly and sang along. I didn't want to interrupt her groove, her comfort, or her layers coming undone. I sat in silence and enjoyed being in her space. Let me find out she could belt out one of these songs. Karaoke night was next on my list.

"Oh, you are showing out tonight," she declared when I parked at her favorite restaurant.

Khaliyah said she loved this seafood joint but hadn't been here in years. She turned toward me with glistening eyes.

My mind instantly jumped into protector mode. "Kay, what's wrong?"

She shook her head, pressing her lips forward. "It's nothing." She blinked, and tears fell. "But it's everything."

"Talk to me." I unbuckled my seatbelt and took her hands into mine.

"It's just that you listened. Nothing is wrong. You're doing everything right. I've never really experienced this type of attentiveness in my life. I barely mentioned this place, and here we are."

I bit down hard and dropped my head to mask my expression. I was relieved that her tears weren't because of a painful memory or any wrongdoing. Her husband's inattentiveness throughout her marriage disappointed me. No, the shit pissed me off. Every relationship was unique, but come on. How the fuck did a man have the privilege of loving her and not do it well, at least for a little while?

As much as I wanted to know everything and fix it for her, I couldn't. All I could do was show her the love and attention she needed now. The past was gone and served its purpose. The present and future were my concern. I wanted to be a part of both in her life. I wanted her in mine.

I needed her in mine.

TWENTY-NINE

Khaliyah

I CALLED Karina as soon as I finished showering. It was a long one. I kept playing the end of our night over and over in my head. I was mad at myself for crying in the car before dinner. Yet, he handled me with so much care. The embarrassment was worth it.

Once inside, someone led us to a somewhat private section. It wasn't in a separate room, but still allowed privacy from the other guests. Airen left his hat in the car. People stared at him, some with wide eyes. The hat did wonders concealing his identity because some people noticed him in its absence. I was honored that he put himself out there for me.

The food was so much better than I remembered. PopPop used to bring me there when I was in high school. Gammy wasn't a restaurant person, so we'd have our grandfather-granddaughter dates once a week. This was our favorite spot.

Over dinner, we talked a bit about my childhood memories of my grandparents raising me. Airen became curious about my parents' whereabouts. For the first time in a long time, I shared what I knew. I never met my father, nor did my grandparents. My mother birthed me while in high school. She wanted to go to college, but didn't believe she was capable because of me. Gammy suggested that they keep me until she graduated. She agreed, but never returned.

The sympathy set in with his demeanor. My grandparents were basically my parents, and I was completely okay with it. I'd learned to accept love where it was given freely and wholeheartedly. I loved my parents and my aunt. They were all I needed to become the woman I am today.

Almost two hours later, we were off to call it a night. It had to end eventually, no matter how good a time we'd had. He pulled into my driveway, and we sat there engaged in a silent conversation with our eyes alone.

"Is it bad that I don't want you to leave?" he asked.

"Same here. We'll see each other soon."

"I know." Airen settled back in his seat, then turned his face toward me.

I examined his features. His neatly trimmed beard covered the lower half of his handsome face. I wanted to kiss each feature my eyes roamed over: his dark brown eyes, wide but cute nose, and pronounced cheekbones. He was flawless, even with what would be considered imperfections.

I couldn't help myself. I placed my palm on his face. Airen's eyes closed with what only seemed like comfort. My eyes welled up again. The peace with this man was overwhelming. I hated when people said "it felt right" with their partner. It seems so far-fetched because of my past. Dammit if I didn't understand it with one touch. Airen felt so right.

I outlined his features with my fingers, desiring nothing more than to kiss him. Almost instantly, his eyes were open and on me. He covered my hand with his and leaned over to me. Coming most of the way, I closed the small space between our lips and pressed mine against his. For a second, I'd stopped breathing. My face became wet at the unrealistic feeling this was. My chest hardly managed to keep my heart in place.

Airen pulled away, looking at me as if he'd been in my head the whole time. His free hand held my cheek as he drew near, connecting us through our lips. My lower center refused to remain calm or let me make all the decisions. Instead, I separated my lips, pulling his bottom one into my mouth. Our slow kiss turned carnal as we introduced our tongues. His hand slowly slid down my arm to my waist, where he squeezed. It was how he showcased his restraint.

I pulled away to remove the temptation to go further. The throbbing between my legs became painful. "I should go inside."

"Yeah," he said with a slow breath. "You should." He pulled himself closer to his side of the car. "Khaliyah, you got me. I have no other words for it. First date or not, you got me. I will give you anything you want. All I ask is that you please be gentle with my heart. I will be gentle with yours. If this is not what you want, say it. We've both experienced love and heartbreak before. I need to know if I am worth your eventual love before I give myself to you. Before I show you my scars and flaws, can I trust you to always be honest with me? No matter what."

My tears revived at his raw vulnerability. "This was one hell of a first date, huh?" I asked because I had no words. He said what I'd felt before we got here. He smiled and stared at me with hope and fear. "I promise to be honest and careful with you."

Airen placed another gentle kiss on my lips after hearing my answer. We'd been in this learning phase for months. Our first official date became more like a confirmation of us being on the same page in pursuit of love. Genuine, healing, forgiving, faithful, unfailing love. A statement that we were together. Society's standards had no say; only we did. We were speaking the same language — acceptance of the inevitable.

I shared my night with Karina because if I hadn't, I wasn't sure I'd believe it actually happened. She cried on the other end of my phone, and then she told me she'd call me right back.

I hadn't realized I'd fallen asleep until my phone rang with Karina's name across the screen. After swiping the green button, all I heard was her voice. "I'm unlocking your front door now. Don't panic. It's me."

My house alarm beeped until she entered the code. Less than a minute later, she was in my bed, lying across from me in her pajamas.

"That explains why it took you thirty minutes to call me back."

"I had no words, boo. I just wanted to be here with you. What's on your heart right now? Your puffy eyes are only telling one side of the story."

I smiled, exhausted from happy tears. The second I spoke, they were coming again. "Man, I never believed I'd be back in this place. Not that I didn't want it. I just…"

"You were over it," she finished what I couldn't. Karina propped herself up on her elbow. "I get that. This is different."

Nodding quickly. "It is. At the same time, it doesn't seem real." I wiped my face with my pajama top. "All of my fears about being used goods and thinking who would love me and my kids the way we deserve made me not care anymore."

"I hate it when you say that, Khaliyah. You are not used goods. Just because one fool couldn't see your worth doesn't mean you have none."

"What if I can't give him what he needs? What if Chris—"

"Aht, shut up. I won't even let you finish speaking that nigga's name in this moment. It is not about him. He made his choice. He felt like you failed him, then okay. You know the part you played and why you made the choices you made. But what you won't do is allow a man who verbally abused you with lies for years to creep into a beautiful time in your life. Let him move on with his wife, and you do the same with your kids and *your* husband. Let's call a thing that be not as though it were. Airen is your husband."

"How about we get to our second date first? But I hear you. Thank you."

"You're welcome. Girl, I'm so glad I pulled up on you. I knew you'd somehow try to turn on yourself. When God gifts you a good thing, accept it. Don't tell God why you don't deserve it. He called you worthy. Therefore, you will always and forever be worthy. Airen recognizes who you are and he ain't no fool. I mean, with all he'd said on the first date, he sees you."

The more I moved forward, the more my thoughts turned against me. All the truths my family and bestie poured into me leaked out when I entertained the lies. I knew better, yet it was a battle I didn't always win. It seemed like an active fight I'd encounter occasionally.

I remained silent, focusing on positive thoughts, and let Karina's words sink in. All the lies I told myself were to hide my shame. It wouldn't hurt to be alone if I convinced myself that no one would want me. I wasn't lonely. I had my babies. I had no expectations of a future love.

Karina spoke into the brief silence. "Accept it and move freely into the blessing before you."

I reached out into the air and grabbed hold of nothing and everything. "I accept."

THIRTY

Airen

DINNER with my aunt and uncle became bearable again after they learned about me dating Khaliyah. We even gave in on Maya's double date invite for Black Love Day — the day before Valentine's Day. She went all out with the food, decor, and itinerary. We had a good time once the woman got her giddy self under control.

Aunt Maya reeled in her excitement yet planned our future before we settled on the thought of truly having one to look forward to. My previous resolve of it simply being me and my daughter was enough until now.

How could the sight of a stranger change the entire trajectory of your life in an instant? How could it alter every accepted possibility you've prepared for? Khaliyah's existence was the one thing I did not consider. Ashtyn, Aydyn, and Aubrey, either.

Family blending never crossed my mind after I walked away from my past a few years ago. One connection obliterated what I'd set in stone. One thing about stone...under the right circumstances, it could shatter.

The capacity of my mind and heart expanded to fit four more. The places that only my little girl occupied now included an entire family. My family. I wanted them more than anything. Ariyah didn't make it any easier. She talked about them constantly. I couldn't escape the longing for a houseful of people I'd die for. People I'd do anything for. Khaliyah's presence bringing peace was nothing but God.

Never had I imagined He'd send a woman into my life as an answer to prayers. All I wanted was peace and happiness. My intentions were about my choices to retreat from everyone. However, every step forward pulled me out of the hole that I asked God to allow me to be content in.

His answer was better.

After dinner, Ariyah and Maya went outside to paint, and I joined Unc in his office.

"I think this is it," I told Uncle Rochon as I dropped myself on the couch. He handed me a quarter-filled glass from his drink cabinet. I took a sip and blew it out slowly.

"Damn, son. You're gone already. Not that she isn't worth it. I distinctly remember you saying how much you'd never fall in love again."

"Didn't you always tell me God laughed at my plans, anyway?"

"I did. Now we see why."

"Unc, I don't know what to even say about it. Something is calming with her, like everything is okay. No matter what chaotic thoughts I had before, hearing her voice or seeing her smile... Even with Mercy, it was never like this."

"Sounds like you've made up your mind. All I gotta say is you take things slow and be careful with her heart. If you fuck with Maya Victoria or her family, it's game over for you. I ain't gone be able to save you. Even though you're family, Khaliyah is protected more than you are."

"Damn, Unc. How many warnings am I going to get? I know how to treat a woman with love and respect. I won't fuck up a damn thing with her. Khaliyah is good with me."

"That's what I like to hear." He reached out and dapped

me up. "You're finally about to have a big family. If I'm not mistaken, it's the exact number of kids you claimed you wanted years ago. You ready for that?"

"It's scary to imagine going from one kid to four, all because I'm falling for her, but she has good kids. I'm not worried at all. I love them. I can teach them so much and support them in ways I'm slowly learning their father hasn't."

"That's a shame. The man was in the same house with his boys and hadn't taught them a damn thing about being a man. Khaliyah was vocal about that part of her marriage. Her grandfather and I made it our business to stand in the gap. I believe one day, he will have a wake-up call. Until then, we're here. And now so are you." Uncle Rochon cleared his throat and brushed his hand down his face. "It seems like you know a bit about her ex. Have you talked to her about Mercy?"

My chest tightened at his words. My focus on the future didn't require picking at that particular scab. "Not yet."

His gaze didn't back down from mine, beckoning him not to travel this road right now. Unc swallowed more of the contents in his glass. "She hasn't asked?"

"Of course, she has."

"What did you tell her?"

"The truth. Mercy's gone."

"Airen?"

"Unc, we will talk about it when it's time. Right now, we're focusing on other things. On us. On a future we both realize we deserve. That's all I want."

He exhaled through his nostrils only. "All I'll say is to be open and honest. It's part of your healing journey. She deserves to know your story, too."

"Khaliyah will get everything she deserves and more from me. We have a lifetime to learn everything about each other. We'll take our time and go at the pace we need to go."

"If you truly believe she is it for you, what's stopping you, son? Transparency and communication are key. You aren't giving her the chance to be there for you fully if you keep this from her."

"I won't." Moments passed while my thoughts traveled to what such a discussion would look like. That part of my life didn't matter anymore. It couldn't touch me because it no longer existed. She no longer existed. Talking about it with the woman I now wanted to share my life with felt pointless. I'd moved on. Looking back for the sake of sharing meant nothing if healing had already taken place.

If you're healed, why are you angry?

I took the last swig of my drink and stood. "I'ma head out, Unc."

"You're leaving because I'm trying to tell you the truth?"

"If that's how you want to take it. I got shit to do." Hiding my disdain served no purpose. I understood where my uncle came from. He had a successful marriage, and I'd be a fool to dismiss wise counsel. However, tonight I didn't have it in me to oblige.

Unc nodded and shrugged. "I guess I'll see you around."

"Yeah. Good night."

I got Ariyah settled into the car and drove us home. The entire ride, my chest was tight. There were things I wasn't quite ready to share. None of it mattered in my relationship with Khaliyah. Pieces of my past didn't belong in my present.

Until it became necessary to discuss, I'd leave it alone. Khaliyah respected my wishes because she trusted me. She knew about my heartbreak. We briefly discussed my family's loss, but not in detail. Not the kind Unc wanted me to release. Speaking on any of it meant speaking on all of it.

I wasn't ready to go there.

KHALIYAH HAD the pleasure of enduring a game night with the clan I'd grown to love. The Harris sisters, their husbands, and friends. A living room full of loud ass, silly adults with good food, games, and conversations. Khaliyah and August were damn near attached at the hip. Frequently throughout the night, the men and women separated. It eased my spirit to see my lady fit right in.

Victor handed me another beer from the fridge as we hung around the kitchen. The women were on the back porch. I could hear Khaliyah's infectious cackle along with the rest of them.

"I see you, Airen!" We tapped bottles. "She's great, man. Nina gave me the nod halfway through the night. If her mean ass likes her, you got a good one."

"I do." I leaned on the counter, resting my elbows there. "It's surreal."

Victor nodded. "Yeah, life is like that sometimes. It makes all the decisions for you and tells you who's boss. Especially when you are dead set on the very opposite of what God had planned."

"Exactly! The crazy thing is that we both found home in a whole new way by changing our location."

"Hearts and minds, too." Victor knew all too well. "It all fell in line when we surrendered our personal pursuits and allowed His to take over."

"The accuracy, brother."

"I'm happy for you." His regard went to the patio door where his wife was. "We've had some shake-ups in life. Thank God for not forgetting the good guys."

"Amen," I agreed, clanking bottles again.

Everyone began filing out after another couple of hours. We said our goodbyes before walking down the sidewalk toward my home. Khaliyah's hand squeezed mine. I slowed to match her strides. "You good?" I asked.

"I am." Her smile wasn't as convincing. We lingered until her small strides resumed. "Can I ask you a question? You don't have to answer it if you don't want to."

A lump suddenly arose in my throat. My heart had already warned me where this was going. I nodded despite my desire not to.

"What happened between you and Mercy?"

Clenching my jaw, I tried to remain calm. Part of me wanted to ask if my uncle put her up to this. As if she read my thoughts, she explained, "August mentioned her a few times when we were outside. Mostly comparisons, which made it clear they weren't close. She made a statement about Mercy hurting you severely. We never really talk about it."

Mentally, I sensed God wanted this conversation to happen. I'd dismissed it with my uncle days ago, and here it was again. I settled my thoughts to speak calmly. "Mercy and I wanted different lives. She loved the spotlight, drama, and other things. I was the opposite. I loved the game, but it cost my family much more than I was willing to pay. I stepped away for the sake of my family. By the time I'd made that choice, Mercy was already gone."

"Are you comfortable sharing how she died?"

"Not really. I'm surprised you haven't looked it up for yourself."

"It's tempting, but I want to know you the old-fashioned way. I don't need a blog to share something from your past that you aren't ready to share with me first. I will wait on you."

"I appreciate it, Khaliyah. I'm not trying to be sneaky or hide things from you. It was a bizarre time in my life. I'd done everything to protect Ariyah from it. Unfortunately, as she gets older, others may expose her to partially true stories.

"That has to be difficult."

"The thought definitely is."

"I'll be here for you when the time comes."

"Thank you, babe. Truly."

"Of course."

I raised her hand to my lips and kissed it several times. Grateful was the only word that came to mind. One day, I'd explain my pain. Today wasn't the day. Being in Khaliyah's presence and knowing how much she cared about my peace was all I needed. August may have opened her big mouth tonight, but she had one thing right. Khaliyah was incomparable to any other woman. She was a gem. A gem a man had in his possession and dismissed her value.

Thank God for fools.

THIRTY-ONE

Khaliyah

"Karina!" I whined. "What am I gonna do with this man?" I collapsed sideways on my couch, helplessly in love as if experiencing this emotion for the first time.

"Marry him, then do every nasty thing that comes to mind, and then do it for the rest of your lives."

I agreed with every word she'd said, but what came out was different. "Hell no! Things could flip on me. I can't let that happen again."

"Girl, if you don't shut your dumb ass up."

I pushed myself to sit up straight. Then I fell to her side and leaned on her shoulder. "I'm scared. He's too good to be true. It makes me wonder when the other shoe will drop on my head, make me put it on, then kick his ass with it. I don't want that to happen."

"Khaliyah, I get that, truly. But, boo, there is nothing to fear except a lifetime without him. I said it before, and I'll say it again since you keep acting like you're stuck on stupid. God has given you a gift. A reward even. You tried your best to be the greatest wife of all time. The thing is, you did it for the wrong man. He didn't want a wife. He only wanted a business partner to make money with. Alren wants you. Do not let your fears block the one man you've been waiting for. The one you deserve and deserves you."

As much as I wanted to rebut every word Karina spoke, I couldn't. Instead, tears left my eyes at the possibility that Airen was the person I could spend the rest of my life with.

Months ago, I retired my heart when it came to loving another man. I was done. When my first go at it came crashing down, I was content with the blessing of being a mother.

Airen Landry, a freaking former NFL player, rushed in and tackled my mindset on love. Ariyah and Aubrey coached him to make the play, and he did it flawlessly. He didn't put on a front to impress me. The man was simply himself. He was everything my aunt and his uncle said he was, and more. He'd healed from some heart traumas of his own and faced his fears to pursue me.

Why me?

Then again, why not me?

I was worth being loved intensely and unconditionally. I thought I'd missed my opportunity because I spent fifteen years with the wrong person. Time mattered in life. The choices we made contributed to the time spent or even wasted. If we stay faithful to God, He will work it out for our good. This was not what I had in mind for my good, but I'd gladly take it.

"Khaliyah?" Karina broke the silence as our movie played. "I see that you're all in love and will do the right thing and tell him soon. However, I have a serious question about Airen."

I lifted my head and faced Karina. "Okay. What is it?"

The seriousness of her expression scared me a bit. I braced myself when she opened her mouth. "Does he have any single friends? I'm ready for a happily ever after, too."

I pushed her shoulder. "I freaking hate you."

She got the giggles, mocking my face when she asked her

question. "I'm for real, though. I be listening to the podcast. If Airen works with former players, how can I get me one?"

"You stupid." I got up and went to my wine fridge in the kitchen. "If you want the answer to that question, ask him. I've met three of his closest friends, and two are happily married."

"Oooh, that leaves one. I like my odds."

"Yeah, I don't. Izak is...a mess."

"Well, shit, call me the cleaner."

I almost spilled the wine I was pouring. I had to put the bottle down and hold on to the counter. She hopped to her feet and started dancing with cleaning moves. This fool acted like she was sweeping and wiping imaginary surfaces.

She met me at the island. "Girl, I will get his ass all the way together. Where he at?"

"Arizona."

"Oh, we gotta change that."

"I'm sure you'll find a way."

"I sure the hell will. Izak is the funny one on their show. Just my type."

"Yeah, because yo ass is silly."

AIREN'S HOUSE was like my second home. He'd picked me up from my house and brought me to his. After parking in his garage next to his other cars, he opened the door for me and helped me out of the car. His lips blessed my neck with a soft kiss.

"I got a surprise for you." Airen held me from behind, allowing his obvious physical attraction to me to press against my lower back. I stood there longer than planned.

After almost three months of dating, we hadn't made love.

He wanted us to be at a certain level before we became intimate, and I loved him more for it.

Sex could distort one's perception of reality and make people believe they love someone because of physical intimacy. Brandy said it in her song. She ain't never lied. Airen cared enough to protect us from a distorted view of where we were in our relationship. Appreciating his stance didn't make it any easier.

"Khaliyah," his voice dragged my name.

It woke me up from my trance. "Hmm."

"We gotta go inside," his voice rumbled slowly.

"Okay." I stepped forward as he walked behind me, never distancing our bodies.

When we reached the door, he kissed my ear. "Close your eyes."

"What are you up to?" I looked up at him behind me.

"If you listen, you'll find out."

"Ugh, fine." I did as instructed. I felt his hand wave in front of my face. "They're closed," I insisted.

"Good."

Airen's body brushed against mine as he went ahead of me and pulled me the rest of the way into his home. An aroma of mouth-watering seafood permeated the air.

After a couple of turns, we reached the porch. The warmth of the air gave it away.

"Open your eyes," was all I heard before doing what he'd said.

My mouth fell open at the balloons, gifts, and picnic setup. "Airen?" I whined with a sliver of irritation.

"Yeah."

Speaking through my teeth, I asked, "What's all this?"

He tugged at my arm, leading me to the table with wine glasses and a bottle on ice. A black-and-white checkered tablecloth covered the outdoor coffee table. Giant pillows were on each side. I lowered myself onto the side he took me to.

"An appreciation date," he finally answered.

"For what? I didn't do anything."

Airen knew how much I valued the little things. It would take serious effort for this man to do "little." He was a big giver and always so thoughtful, with a healthy serving of going overboard. Mr. Airen was the overboard king regarding the people he cared about. As much as I hated being spoiled, I loved that about him. I'd get over it eventually and just let him do him.

"Woman!" He sat on the outdoor sofa behind me and held my hands. "You've done so much without trying, I don't know if I could handle what your intentional effort looks like. You've changed my heart by simply being you. My life is lighter and promising. Ariyah has a lifelong best friend at five." He laughed at that one. Those girls have been inseparable. They were with Aunt Maya and Karina now. "You've opened me up to a life I called impossible."

"Aww, babe." I reached for his neck so I could kiss him. Once our lips touched, my eyes welled.

Airen kissed my hands. "Khaliyah, these past few months of dating and learning you have been some of my life's most fulfilling, eye-opening moments. I believed it would be me and Ariyah until she grows up and leaves the nest. Then it'd be only me. I had no desire to love anyone else after Mercy. I didn't think my heart could handle the risk of another devastating heartbreak.

"I never thought I could trust another woman with my heart again. That motherfucker floated on into your hands the moment I met you and didn't let me in on the plan until it was too late. I cannot explain the certainty in my soul, but I will not deny what I feel with you, about you, and whenever I'm near you.

"You stay on my mind. I see a future with you. I get visions of our lives together—all of us. Your kids are mine and mine is yours. So, this day marks three months since you agreed to let me in. I will never take it for granted. You fought against your fears and allowed me to show you what we can be together. I have no doubts. I want to shower you with love, gifts, and anything your heart desires within my capabilities. I will go to God for the things that are not. I got you today and for as long as you let me."

Airen's head dropped, but I could see his smile and the resolve in his features. "I love you, Khaliyah. I have fallen hard for you. I never want to get up. You are it for me and my daughter. She claimed you the first time she saw you."

I laughed nervously. "I remember that," I whispered. My voice was gone, and my emotions were all jumbled up from his confession. "Are you sure you want to take on a family of four, though?" I asked to be funny but also remind him what that meant.

Airen kissed his teeth and tilted his head to the side. "That ship has sailed, woman. To ease your mind, stating the obvious, yes, I am sure. A million times over."

My chest almost hurt at the pace of my heart. Every thought was on the verge of being verbalized. Letting it out would only solidify the inevitable and make it real. "I have to admit I love you, too. It will eat at me if I don't get it off my chest. It's hard to release it into the atmosphere after seeing what trusting those feelings did to both of us. It's even harder to ignore what every part of me understood when you walked into my life."

One blink had tears rolling down my man's face. My man. *God, it felt good.*

Airen placed his hands on my cheeks and planted his soft lips on mine again. I positioned myself between his legs to wrap my arms around his neck as our tongues got acquainted.

The warmth of my body caused slight perspiration. The deepening of our connection at our mouths pulled muffled moans from both of us.

He pulled away and pecked my forehead, nose, and lips one more time. "I have more to show you."

"Airen, you are spoiling me." I pouted. Being the usual gift giver in relationships, I'd need time and practice receiving without complaining.

"Not even close. This is a tiny token of all I will give you and our babies."

The butterflies fluttered away at his acceptance of my—I mean, our kids. Even if not by blood, I was sure they'd want nothing more.

"Well, I do smell something heavenly."

"That's because I cooked you a little something. So, sit back and relax on your throne in my house and my heart. I'll be back." With one more kiss, he'd left me outside.

God, is this real? I'm not dreaming, am I?

I pinched myself and happily accepted the pain. Airen Landry was officially mine, and I was his. Not on paper, but in the way that mattered the most.

A few minutes passed before he rolled a wooden cart to the table. He placed a mouthwatering bowl of shrimp and grits topped with a creamy sauce, charred sausage, and bacon. Mr. Landry was going to be a problem if this tasted as good as it looked. He set a plate with toasted garlic bread between us.

"Oh, you tryna GTD," I said.

"When the time is right." He winked and sat opposite me.

Airen prayed over the food and waited for my first bite. "Nigga," was all that came out as my eyes closed.

He laughed, nodding his head. "I told you I know what I'm doing."

Oh, he was trying to trap me. I had no qualms about any of it.

THIRTY-TWO

Airen

I'D LOST count of how many times Khaliyah and the kids have been over. These days, I wish they never had to go home. Granted, I understood how important it was for Khaliyah to have a home she worked her ass off to get. Selfishly, I wanted her to drop it all and live with us.

First, I'd have to convince her we were worth another trip down the aisle. My heart and soul had immediately chosen her. My mind took a minute to get on board. Rightfully so. I'd only given my heart to two women in the past. Both mishandled it. Something in me knew Khaliyah would handle me with care, just as she does my daughter and her family.

Seeing the example in her interactions chipped away at the negative thoughts. The many possible endings dwindled down to only one: completion. A missing piece I denied needing fulfilled now urged me to make it happen for our lifetime.

After handing Khaliyah a glass of one of her favorite wines, I sat close to her. Even the subtlest touch eased me. God covered this woman with a type of peace I couldn't comprehend. He'd given me the honor of receiving it in her presence.

"What's on your mind, Airen? You're so quiet today."

Thinking about how to make you mine forever. "Wondering what our kids are up to."

She smiled. "Leave it to my boys to make small activities memorable. Whatever they do will be super cute."

"Y'all are something else. How did you teach them to be so attentive and caring at such a young age? Aydyn is unlike any middle child I'd ever met. No brat bone in his body."

Khaliyah burst out laughing. "You noticed that too?" She raised one hand in the air. "That is nothing but God. I cover my kids in prayer daily, but God is in control. I follow His lead and reap the reward. I prayed for wisdom and discernment with every move I made as a parent. I didn't want to mess it up. Especially when I met their father's true form. My ultimate goal was to minimize his influence on them. So far, so good. Praise Jesus!"

I watched her sip the wine, close her eyes, and push out a long breath. Wondering what that meant, I asked God to help me be the type of man who would always be a positive influence on her children. I never wanted to become someone she'd have to shield them from.

Ashtyn walked downstairs and approached us wearing a suit jacket over his pajamas. Khaliyah's eyes lit up before her laughter filled the room, causing me to do the same.

"Boy, what do you have on? I didn't see you bring—" She narrowed her eyes at her son. "What are y'all up to?"

"If you would please follow me, kind sir and kind ma'am, you will find out," Ashtyn said with a bow.

Khaliyah and I locked eyes before I helped her to her feet. We followed behind her son until he stopped at the game room's entrance. Ashtyn gestured for us to enter, and we followed his subtle instruction.

Everyone, semi-dressed up, stood next to the TV, displaying a picture of the six of us. The bold letters above the image read: Our Future Together.

We sat where directed by Aydyn. For five minutes, we listened to an impressively well put-together presentation.

They hooked a laptop to my TV using an HDMI cord that didn't belong to me. Ashtyn even used a clicker for each slide transition.

Each of our kids had a part as if they had rehearsed it for some time. No one missed a mark. Their performance astonished me. I clocked Khaliyah wiping a few tears between the slides.

The premise of their message was their reasoning on why Khaliyah and I should fall in love and get married. When they finished, I stood and clapped.

"So, what do y'all think?" Aydyn asked.

"My first question is, who taught y'all how to make a professional presentation?" I asked with genuine curiosity.

Ashtyn pointed at Khaliyah. "Mom did when she home-schooled us. We learned way more than the kids at school."

I slow clapped for my amazing woman, who, according to his presentation, should be my wife soon. I had no arguments.

"Kudos to you, Kay," I told her. "That was impressive."

Ariyah stood with a smile and interlocked her fingers with Aubrey's. Her smile was equally beautiful and convincing.

Khaliyah was still in a bit of a daze. The same amazement I felt. I reclaimed my seat beside her and nudged her to say something. After a few more moments passed, the woman finally opened her mouth. "I have no words," she said. "How did y'all...when did y'all put this together?"

"A couple of weeks ago. We practiced when we played at Mr. Airen's house," Aydyn answered.

"Wow!" Khaliyah expressed. "While I understand why you'd want this union to happen, marriage is very serious business. It's not something anyone should jump into lightly or for all the good feelings. Airen and I—"

"Will consider the possibility," I finished for her. I squeezed her hand, which rested next to mine on the sectional, and stopped her rebuttal. "Let them have this moment," I whispered.

Khaliyah smiled at me with narrowed eyes and looked back at the kids. "It's a maybe for me," she replied.

The cheers from all four of our children were a hint that we needed to get on board. They convinced me, but, as Khaliyah said, we both knew this wasn't a decision to take lightly. We'd both been down this road once, unsuccessfully. If we'd travel it again, it had to be done right and with our full commitment.

Ashtyn and Aydyn asked Khaliyah and me to leave yet again. They needed time to set up for their next surprise. We rolled with it. The boys knew where everything was in my house and ran around as such. Their devices automatically hooked up to my Wi-Fi and printer. They changed my password from the generic one that came with the box. I never personalized it all these years, but they came along and settled right in. I had no complaints.

I led my lady outside to sit on the balcony and wait for whatever else our kids had in store. Even thinking about "our" kids made it feel so official.

We took a seat on the bench swing. Khaliyah rested her head on my shoulder. "I guess that means we'll get pre-marital counseling soon."

My entire body shifted so that I could see her face. *Was she serious?*

"What?" she looked as if she didn't say something life-changing.

I narrowed my eyes at hers. "Babe, are you for real?"

"I'm not proposing, and you'd better not either. I want to see if we are ready for a lifetime together or if we're on the same page with our life's goals and vision with the help of a professional. I made that mistake the first time and will not repeat it."

"Whatever you want, Kay. That's all you will ever hear from me. We are on the same page."

"Boy, you don't know that for sure. We need someone to guide us. I can't mess this up again, Airen. I won't survive another divorce."

"That won't be a thing. If we ever jump the broom, it cannot be undone. We'd have to work through whatever comes at us."

"Jumping the broom, huh?"

"Yep! My grandmother kept the one from our family."

"Shut up! Is it the same one that Aunt Maya and Rochon used?"

"It is. Mercy refused, so we didn't. I'm not taking no for an answer the next time."

"You said whatever I wanted, though."

I jerked my head back at her already using my words against me. "That's after we jump the broom, woman."

She burst out laughing. "I would love that, Airen."

"Let's set a date then."

Her laughter filled my ears again. "Slow your roll. Counseling first. A proposal, second. Then maybe an acceptance before we get to the broom."

"Whatever you want."

THIRTY-THREE

Khaliyah

ARIYAH AND AUBREY were wearing me the hell out today. It was all part of the day's plan, but it was barely two in the afternoon. Everything in me regretted not bringing Karina along. Two five-year-old girls didn't seem like a lot when I promised them a girls' day. It was their birthday weekend.

The family joked that we were truly meant to be together since our daughters were born on the exact same day within the same hour. The girls wanted a day with me and a night with all of us. Tomorrow, on their actual birthday, we'd have a family pool party at Airen's with everybody else. We made sure to book Cherished Memories and Treats by Leah B. for the occasion.

So far today we've checked off breakfast at a restaurant, time at the park, nails and toes painted, Chuck E. Cheese for games and lunch, and now shopping. Airen put money in my account because Ariyah begged for this day. I didn't argue with him. Airen and his daughter weren't ones to back down when they wanted something. It may be subtle, but they could be demanding.

Our girls' day meant he'd have a guys' day with my sons. I smiled at the thought of them together having a ball. My boys were sweet, but honest with their feelings. With Airen, they were home. The man was a big ass kid right along with them. They loved being around him, and it kept them from getting on my nerves. My boys were full of so much energy. I hated going outside all the damn time. Airen didn't. He came at the right time in our lives.

For our shopping leg of the day, we went to the mall. Our first stop was the bookstore. We each came out with a handful of books in a bag. We shopped in a cute kiddie shoe store and then a candy store. The girls had to promise to wait until later to eat any of the candy we bought. By the time the girls and I entered the next store, I heard the magic words from my baby, "Mommy, I'm tired."

"Me, too," Ariyah added.

My arms almost shot up in the air to give all glory to God. I didn't want to be the one to cut this short. I would've gone on as long as they wanted to. Our expected return was in a couple of hours. Airen planned for us to finish the night with dinner at Oliver's Grill.

"Do you want to leave now?" I hoped they did.

"Can we get a bear first?" Ariyah asked in the middle of the Build-A-Bear store. I gave her a look she understood well. "Please?" she poked her lip out before cheesing ear-to-ear.

"Sure. We're already here," I folded.

"Yay!" she and Aubrey cheered.

Twenty minutes, too many damn accessories for stuffed bears, and a quick line later, I paid for our things and we were finally ready to go. As we walked out of the store's entrance, Aubrey's shoe became untied again. She'd been tying it all day.

I set the bags down with my arms in the loops to tie my baby's shoe. Out of nowhere, a woman approached Ariyah, wrapping her arms around her. "It's you! Baby Doll, I found you."

"The fuck!" I pushed the woman away and off of Ariyah. "Don't touch her."

Ariyah grabbed onto my leg and held me with all her might. She looked in the opposite direction from the woman.

"The hell is wrong with you. Don't grab my child like that!"

The woman straightened up and stood there. Something about her was familiar, but I couldn't put my finger on it.

"I'm so sorry. I thought she was—"

"No! Hell no. You don't grab someone's kid for any reason," I yelled. I took both girls by the wrists and pulled them along with me. Neither of them said a thing. They kept up with my pace as we rushed through the mall and past people to get to my car. I kept looking back subtly. I didn't want to freak the girls out as much as I was.

The same woman was near us in the bookstore, too. I figured that's why she seemed familiar. She'd been watching us. Was she waiting for an opportunity to take Ariyah?

I got the kids into the car, and their faces gave away their fear. Once we were on the road, I had to say something. "We're okay, girls. I'm sorry for being loud with that woman earlier. She scared me. She should never have touched you, Ariyah."

"I'm not hurt, Ms. Khaliyah. She hugged me."

"I know, baby. It still scared me. There are too many people who do bad things in the world. No stranger should ever do that, even if it was a hug. You understand?"

"Yes." Ariyah dropped her eyes to something I couldn't see from the rearview mirror.

It played repeatedly in my head: her pixie haircut, peanut butter skin, slim figure, and tatted neck. It was a butterfly or something. She looked surprised when I told her not to grab my child. Why did my reaction surprise her? Did I know her? Did she know Ariyah? She called her Baby Doll. Or did she say she looked like a baby doll?

My mind moved much faster than my car. The girls were

each looking out their windows. I put my eyes back on the road and continued our commute.

"Anyone want ice cream?" I tried to reel everything back in. Smiles found their way back to my girls' faces.

I made a few turns to get to the ice cream shop I spotted. I had to get myself together before taking Ariyah home and admitting to Airen that a woman could have snatched his daughter right before my eyes. He may never trust me again. No one should have gotten that close to her, let alone "hug" her. I felt awful.

Inside, Ariyah held my hand tighter than before, but she seemed back to normal otherwise. We ordered ice cream and took a seat at a table.

I needed to say something to keep the girls calm yet gauge how Ariyah was feeling. That shit was scary for me, so I could only imagine how a five-year-old felt. Even though I kept her safe, more happened than I was comfortable accepting.

"You like your ice cream?" I asked as Ariyah licked away at her single scoop.

She nodded quickly. "It's yummy."

"Mine too, Mommy," Aubrey chimed in. "I love cotton candy."

"So much so, you never want to change it up," I pointed out.

Aubrey giggled at the truth. She shared the memory of her brothers picking ice cream for each other and how silly they acted with the flavors. She reenacted her big brothers, gagging at the combination of what they knew the other wouldn't like.

Ariyah laughed so much she had to stop eating her ice cream. My baby did her best to take Ariyah's mind off what happened. She went into protective mode for her buddy. She would do it whenever she thought anyone was sad or upset. As usual, it worked.

I took it as my cue to leave it alone and talk with Airen

when we returned to his house. In my mind, dinner was canceled. A stranger got close enough to grab his daughter in my care. A gorgeous stranger who seemed like she knew Ariyah. I couldn't shake that part. Was it a mistaken identity? Did she think Ariyah was someone else?

Why did I feel like I'd seen her? Even before the bookstore. *Lord, if I'm right, show me.*

The girls played and talked about nothing as we finished our dessert. When I finally let go of the topic, Aubrey told Ariyah, "Mommy is a Mama Bear. She will always protect us."

Ariyah's smile grew, then dissipated. "Mommy. She looked like my mommy," she said as though just remembering. "But my mommy is in heaven."

Immediately, it clicked. That's where I remembered the woman from. My skin crawled and itched with anger.

He lied to me.

He lied to his daughter.

He lied.

THIRTY-FOUR

Airen

I SET up a surprise for Ashtyn and Aydyn today. We'd have our guys' day with some extra people they weren't expecting. Ariyah woke up earlier than expected and helped me make breakfast for the boys, since the ladies were going out for breakfast. As soon as my lady walked through the door, I darted to her for a kiss because I knew Ariyah wouldn't want to waste a minute of her girls' day.

"I will see you later," was all I got out after our lips briefly touched. Ariyah pushed me toward the kitchen for my day to start so she could get to hers.

Khaliyah rested her hand on her hip as we watched my daughter grab Aubrey's arm with one hand and the other on the doorknob. "Oh, baby girl is ready to go."

"She went to sleep early to get to this part quicker." I laughed and walked the ladies to Khaliyah's truck. I snuck in one more kiss before watching them leave.

Once inside, Ashtyn had already started eating the fruit. "Just couldn't wait, huh?"

He raised his hands in defense. "I only took a grape."

"Let's finish up, then we can eat." I checked on the bacon, which was almost done in the oven. I poured more batter into the waffle maker. "Take the orange juice and apple juice out and set them on the table for me."

Aydyn jumped at the request and did what I'd asked. When he set it down, I noticed the confusion on his face. "Hey, Airen, why are there so many plates?"

"I have a few more men coming over. Uncle Rochon should be at the gate now. And Victor is heading over with his oldest son."

"Really?" Ashtyn asked. "Maybe he can show us how to get rich like him."

I laughed but had similar hopes. Victor and his firm changed my life financially. My connection with him meant the world to me; he was so generous with his knowledge. Ashtyn and Aydyn would completely benefit from it, depending on their eagerness to learn. Fortunately, Victor learned early from his stepfather, setting him up for life. Being the type of dude he was, he put everyone close to him up on what he'd learned. We're all eating better than most in our position because of him and his dad.

"Whatever he shares with you, listen carefully. That may turn into a sure thing." I winked and watched his mouth drop at the possibility before directing Ashtyn to take the glasses to the table.

When Unc pulled up, I got my phone out and pressed record. The boys were aware of the podcast and who I'd worked with. I warned Khaliyah about the language, so the boys couldn't listen. Thanks to Izak. I had Ashtyn open the door for Uncle Rochon. When he did, the boy took off running through my damn house. I couldn't stop laughing. Aydyn froze with bugged-out eyes.

Nick and Izak were like supermen to these kids. Victor walked in while the door was still open, and his son turned around, heading toward my front lawn. He kept repeating,

"They're not real. That's not real." Victor nodded, and Junior finally came inside and stood in shock next to Aydyn.

"Alright, young men, these are still human beings. Be in that kind of awe with God," Uncle Rochon said. "They are knuckleheads just like y'all. Only older and bigger."

"You *really* know them, know them?" Ashtyn asked. "I thought—I mean, you said..."

Aydyn was the first to wake up from the trance. He offered his hand to Nick first. "It's so nice to meet you, sir." He repeated the same thing with Izak.

Of course, Izak had to dap him up with a bit of rough-housing. "Whaddup, young man! I'm glad you found your voice."

Aydyn smiled. "Yes, sir."

"You making a nigga feel old," Izak told Aydyn.

Unc quickly backhanded Izak in the gut. "Be respectful with your language around impressionable young men. You know better."

"Yes, sir." Izak sounded exactly like Aydyn.

I caught it all on video. Ashtyn slowly made his way down the middle of my foyer, still taking it all in. Junior shook the men's hands and stood quietly next to Victor. This would be a fun experience for us all.

My kitchen was full of black men and boys with a plethora of knowledge and experience, split between us. We ate and talked. The boys asked every question that came to mind, and we answered them all. Their range went from what it was like on the field to the money, fame, and retirement. None of the boys were into sports outside of hobbies, but they still admired what it took to play the game they watched on the screen. Ashtyn picked Victor's brain about being so young when he made his first million. It was a fact I shared because I was there when it happened.

Uncle Rochon got questions from the adults about

marriage and balancing successful businesses. We made the most of our conversation before it was time to play. The guys and I planned to do some drills with the boys for fun. We still had it and every damn thing impressed them. We played tag football and basketball before we swam. Aunt Maya and Victor's wife, Nina, set up our lunch while we built an appetite. They were in and out before I called everyone to eat. We were on a schedule since Izak and Nick had a flight to catch soon.

Mid-afternoon, our guys' day trickled to an end. Uncle Rochon took the boys to drop Izak and Rochon off at the airport. They begged to go. Victor and Junior left soon after, leaving me with a quiet house and enough time to shower before the ladies returned.

I had just descended the stairs when Khaliyah pulled into the garage. I opened the door for them. The girls gave me hugs on the way in. Khaliyah stood at the trunk of her truck, grabbing bags.

"Lemme get that, gorgeous. You can go in and relax. I wanna hear about your day." I leaned in to kiss her cheek since she never faced me. Khaliyah dodged it, moved to the other side of the truck, and went into the house.

I picked up the rest of the bags, closed the trunk, and followed behind her. "What happened? Why you acting like that?"

Khaliyah didn't slow her pace before reaching the living room and dropping everything in her hands: keys, phone, everything. I put what I held down and tried to close the distance between us. She swiftly moved several steps back.

Moments ago, I was excited to tell her all about the successful day with her boys and the fun we had. Now, I wanted to kill whoever put her in this mood.

"Baby, talk to me. What's wrong?" I asked. My next thought was that something had happened with the girls, but they giggled loudly upstairs in Ariyah's room. When her door was open, you could hear everything. I made sure not to be too loud as I questioned my lady again about her sour ass mood. Who the fuck did something to her?

"Khaliyah…You gotta give me something here. I can't help if you won't let me in on what the fuck is going on. Babe, please?"

Khaliyah stood there with her eyes studying me. Her mind seemed occupied, but her focus was on me. She broke away from my eyes and raised her hands to the middle of her stomach, then opened her mouth. Nothing came out. Her face scrunched up in confusion, then disgust.

I clasped my hands behind my back because trying to touch her was out of the question. Every move forward, she'd move backward. Her voice finally made a sound, but no words.

God, what was going on?

"You…" She stopped for a few moments.

"I what, baby? You're scaring me."

Khaliyah laughed with an arrogance that irritated my soul. "Scared? I just saw a fucking ghost. I must have. Because what kind of sick motherfucker would lie about a dead wife? Who would tell his daughter that her mother is in heaven?" She asked calmly. Not loud enough to travel upstairs, but clear enough for my ears.

"Khaliyah, I don't know what you're talking about. Please walk me through this. What is—"

"I saw her, Airen! Your wife is alive and well."

"I think you're mistaken, baby. This all has to be a misunderstanding. You know me."

"I don't know shit, Airen. Your wife approached us at the mall. She was slimmer than in Ariyah's pictures, with shorter hair and a neck tattoo. I'm not crazy. She hugged Ariyah and called her Baby Doll."

It was my turn to freeze in place. My throat instantly lost all moisture.

Tattoo on her neck?

The thought of what Khaliyah described knocked me back a few steps. I placed my hand on my head, massaging my right temple to keep it together.

Everything was finally feeling normal. The past was where it was supposed to be—behind us. I found my forever in the woman before me, yet she'd gotten a glimpse of my past I'd convinced myself I'd outrun. I pushed it far down in my mind so I could be happy again, but I'd forgotten a major part of why I stayed hidden for so long. Three years wasn't long enough. Yet the short time spent with Khaliyah made it feel like a decade ago.

My chest tightened as the reality of my past came crashing into my future. There was no hiding or turning back now. I didn't want to lose her over this. I didn't lie to her. I only shared what I thought was relevant until now.

I let my knees falter beneath me as my mind filled with memories, mostly bad ones. The promises I'd made to myself when I left Arizona. The walls I'd built around me that Khaliyah successfully shattered. Those walls existed for a reason. Now, everything was exposed. I sat down in silence and dropped my head, trying to wrap my mind around all that could happen from this moment on. Khaliyah slowly approached me, knelt, and shook me. I heard sounds from her mouth, but I couldn't distinguish the words.

I finally opened my mouth and released the one thing that had played continuously in my mind for the last minute.

"She found us."

To be continued...

afterword

Thank you from the bottom to the top of my heart for reading Retired On Love! Feel free to rate and/or review book one of the All or Nothing series. Two more are coming soon.

This was a labor of love, tears, pain, anger, forgiveness, and so many other emotions. Ultimately, healing.

Airen and Khaliyah are from a dream I had two years before my divorce. It took a lot of starting and stopping due to it hitting too close to home. But we're here!

I'm so grateful for your patience and support. A special thank you to Bridgette and Telicia, my fellow Same Book, 3 Time Zones co-hosts. You ladies have been so loving and supportive throughout my writing career. I probably would've let life make me quit writing, but I'm grateful y'all stayed on me to get back to it. Love you!

To my readers, thank you for being open to my stories. Love stories are as complicated as the people in love. My goal is to explore as much of them as my imagination will allow. I appreciate you for taking this ride with me.

REAL BLACK-OWNED BUSINESSES

Cherished Moments & Treats by Leah B. are businesses I have had the pleasure to experience. These young women are extremely talented and I believe in their dreams. If you are in or near Houston, TX - order treats from Leah B. for your Cherished Moments decorated event LOL. I love them!

A LIL PERSONAL BUT... (proud mama moment)

Ashtyn is a character based off of my oldest daughter. The negative parts of this story came from recent events in our lives. Many of the conversations between Khaliyah and Ashtyn were the same ones I'd had with my daughter. It's crazy how much we learn from our babies and how much they see and hear when we think we are protecting them.

My daughter created a poem this past school year for English class and when she read it to me, I almost broke down. She experienced the nightmare with me and there was nothing I could do about it. All I can do is love her through it all and make better decisions as her (and her brother and sister's) provider and protecter.

Anyway, I wanted to share her poem with you AND the animation that went along with it for her project. It was a rush job but it's perfect to me. She's working on becoming an animator and manga creator so this is her work in the beginning stages.

Okay, that's all I got! Stay Blessed.

this is my home

By Angelina

At first it was an apartment that I'll never remember
Then it was my great-grandma's house that I still visit today
After that a small house that's a phantom in my memories
I remember my brother and sister's birth
How excited I was, not understanding how I'd have to protect them
I remember my first sleepover, my first taste of friendship
It was fleeting
I remember the dancing, singing, gaming, and laughing
My happy family, Mom Dad Zoe Ryan and Me
But I also remember the screaming
Let's move on
After that was a freezing apartment in Minnesota
Not many memories
Just my first time seeing snow, going to the park at midnight to play in it
And the false sense of stability it gave
I still remember the screaming...
Then it was a big house in Minnesota
The one I count as my childhood home, even though I've had a ton
Upstairs Mom cooked, we ran around and played without a care in the world
But it was hell...screaming...fighting...throwing things

But let's focus on the positive
Downstairs was a different world
MetaphorToys and tents where we could ignore the commotion upstairs
Dvds and games
An ugly red carpet as soft as a pillow, especially when we built pillow forts
The ignorance couldn't last forever
A fateful night when downstairs became upstairs
Yelling...screaming...breaking doors...blaring music and crazy eyes
Terrified children...a crying mother...a bus ride back to great-grandma's house
Hoping to escape the monster called alcoholism
But let's keep going
My home was my Great-grandma's
Then my aunt
Then the alcoholic (self-proclaimed sober)
We can guess how that ended
Then my Great-grandma as well as a few crackheads
Minnesota was a distant memory, a dream of what home could be
But God is good
Finally free of the monster
Me Mom Zoe Ryan
We made Minnesota our home again
For real
Now it's laughing, gaming, singing, and dancing
Fighting but resolving
Hurting but Forgiving
This is my home

If you're interested in the animation.
https://bit.ly/45Td96x

Renée is from the best city on the planet—Houston. Since Texas is too damn hot, she now resides in Minnesota with her three kids. She writes fiction based on African American characters. Renée loves creating stories with relationship drama that can easily be found in many households. She wants readers to see themselves or recognize someone they know in her characters. If she can make you laugh, gasp, think, or even cry, then her mission will be accomplished.

Connect with Renée:
On Instagram @reneeamoses
On Facebook @authorramoses
www.reneeamoses.com

Listen to Same Book, 3 Time Zones: A Black Book Review Podcast
We read one book a month and post our discussion.
www.sb3tzreviews.com

Signup for latest news, first looks, and exclusive content: bit.ly/RAMList

also by renée a. moses

Turns in Love Series (Complete)

Two Lefts, One Right

Making a Hard Right

Straightaway

Wishing for Her (Christmas Short)

Truth Is...

Harris Sisters Series (Complete)

The Cost of Love You

I Thought I Knew You

Never Stopped Loving You

Not Good Enough For You

I Want It All With You

All or Nothing Series

*Retired On Love**

Standalones

You Could Do Damage

When the Time is Wright (Christmas Novella)

www.ingramcontent.com/pod-product-compliance
Lightning Source LLC
Chambersburg PA
CBHW060714190726
48289CB00002B/679